I just can't let you go

For some, the power of pain works...
For some, it's the power of divine...
For me, it's the power of your love...

MANAH

© **Manah 2020**

All rights reserved

All rights reserved by author. No part of this publication may be reproduced, stored in a retrieval system or transmitted in any form or by any means, electronic, mechanical, photocopying, recording or otherwise, without the prior permission of the author.

Although every precaution has been taken to verify the accuracy of the information contained herein, the author and publisher assume no responsibility for any errors or omissions. No liability is assumed for damages that may result from the use of information contained within.

First Published in May 2020

ISBN: 978-93-90119-09-7

BLUEROSE PUBLISHERS
www.bluerosepublishers.com
info@bluerosepublishers.com
+91 8882 898 898

Cover Design:
Tyngshain Pariat

Typographic Design:
Namrata Saini

Distributed by: BlueRose, Amazon, Flipkart, Shopclues

Acknowledgments

I feel truly special because of the blessings that the almighty has blessed me with. Although I've put in a great deal of enthusiasm into this book, the master has been there with me throughout as my guardian angel.

Apart from the great master, I want to extend my heartfelt gratitude to a few people who have been a constant support throughout my journey of beginning as a writer.

Thanking my parents would be an understatement for the beautiful and most loving parents that they've always been. The way they have raised me to become what I am today, cannot be expressed in words. Love you both. I also owe a lot to my beloved sister Mrs. Siya Bhagwani.

My brother, Vishal Khubchandani, always taught me to aspire for the better. Who not only showed me the correct path but also taught me to walk on it. And the road to writing became much more easier ever since he got married, as I had got an honest reviewer for my book - Mrs. Pehel Khubchandani, my sister by law. She not only reviewed my work but also made me realise that I have the potential to do it. She has been my biggest blessing in every moment of disguise.

I'd like to thank my husband and my in-laws for understanding and accepting my passion, and letting me do things my way.

Special thanks to my brother-in-law Mr. Jack kukreja for sparing time whenever I was in need of assistance, and for boosting my esteem when I felt low.

I'd also like to thank my editor Mrs. Monika Jasuja Amarnani for exactly reading my mind and giving her best to refurbish my work, along with maintaining the originality of my writing.

Café Vivo had been the most suitable and best place for me to write my heart out. This place will always be special to me.

Last but not the least, thanks to my friend Miss. Rachana Waghmare who always showed a true belief in me and who was the first person to make me realise that everyone is special in their own way.

You all have in so many ways done your bit to help me realise this once-a-far-fetched dream of mine.

About the Author

Manah is an aspiring author. Writing was close to her heart ever since she was a child. She loved penning things down right from her school days. Most of the times you will find her pondering over something to write or writing something which she has already thought about. Apart from being a writer, she is a loving mother and a homemaker. Manah feels rather than focusing on the commercial success of the book, even if she could make a mark on a single soul, that means a huge success to her. Its her easy going nature n go with the flow to whatever life offers makes her a pleasant person. You will always find her full of gratitude about everything around her.

January 13, 2018 Saturday afternoon

That particular day his condition seemed much better. That one glimmer of hope was enough to remind me that I could actually smile. Smiling- an act that I had almost forgotten. The series of events in the previous month had reduced and confined me to tears alone. Although I had been visiting him at the hospital daily, the way he reacted on seeing me that day was different from usual. He leapt up from his bed and hugged me. The intensity and swiftness of his hug were enough to make me reel. I lurched but didn't fall; he wouldn't let me. I was in the arms of a strong man. I was in the arms of *my* man. My eyes were still filled with tears but, somehow, the reason was not the same. The tears today held a sense of thankfulness, a sense of pleasure that something better was around the corner. But in the next few moments, I was proven completely wrong. I had missed him and the intimacy we had shared the last few days. Meeting him only to see him in pain was not bearable for me at all, but not meeting him wasn't an option either.

His hands were around my waist, and my fingers were in his hair, caressing them. The only noise I could hear in this sheer silence was his heartbeat which was cracking that day. We had both missed the warmth we felt in each other's arms. It was evident how desperate he was to meet me that day. But the question was, Why? Why all of a sudden?

I finally broke the silence and asked him,

"Is everything okay, baby?"

I was taken aback with his painful response.

"Nidhi, please help me. Please take me out of this... it's getting worse day-by-day. I can't forget her; I can't forget what happened. Her face whirls around in my mind all day long. I seldom sleep, and the moment I fall asleep, her nightmares startle me. How come humans have become so ruthless! Why did that bastard turn a blind eye to Rihanna's condition and run away? Help me, Nidhi! Help me forget this nasty past of mine, or else..."

"Or else?"

"Just let me go... I can't bear this anymore. Please let me go."

Before I could say anything, his mom broke into the room. He stopped talking abruptly. Obviously, he hadn't mustered the courage to confess it before his mother that he wanted to die. That he doesn't feel like living anymore. His mother was already going through a lot. She was the mother of a twenty-two-year-old son who was fighting against his sad reality. The one who was in conflict with his own self. He didn't want to aggravate his mom's pain.

"My dear, please get these medicines prescribed. I've accidentally left my spectacles at home today," his mom said to me.

"Off course, aunty, please give me the prescription," I responded.

I took the prescription from her hand and left. I should have returned within ten minutes, but it took me half an hour instead. I returned with the medicines and a note for Kabir. I left it near his pillow. He noticed me leaving it there.

After giving the medicines to aunty I left for my house.

"Bye, Kabir."

I didn't even wait for him to respond and turned around to leave. After a while, probably when his mother was taking her afternoon nap, he read the note, which said—

I want to be in the dark, but the sun still shines bright...

I want peace, but the streets spurn to stay calm...

I don't feel like eating, but my gut withholds to stay empty...

I want to be left to myself, but am constantly surrounded by people...

I just want to cry my lungs out, but soon the vigour fades and sleep conquers...

I chase peace, but nightmares continue recreating the turmoil...

If something has the power to change me, it's your love...

What brings me from darkness to light is your love...

What brings me from clamour to peace, is your love...

The one who brings butterflies to my stomach is you...

One who always stays with me through thick and thin, is your love...

The one who taught me the art of spreading joy, is you...

What turned my nightmares into beautiful dreams, is your love...

For the sun, moon and the universe will all conspire to make you mine...

You own all my breath till I take the last one...

I can't let you go...

I just can't let you go...

Wednesday, 9:30 a.m. July 12, 2017

Bhai and I were at the breakfast table, sharing a meal and awkward silence. The mild chirping of birds was the only audible sound. Every morning leaving the balcony door open was like a fixed pattern that we followed at home. It let the sunlight and fresh breeze break in which was followed by the melodious sound of birds. We had a very big landscape garden with a large front porch in our countryside holiday home. It was named 'Miraaj' after combining the names of our parents, Meera and Raj. We always stayed there whenever we visited Pune. The house had a home garden in the front and at the back, there was a spacious parking lot. Our parking lot was one of a kind and had the best cars to its shelter. Miraaj was a combination of opulence and emotions. My mother's touch added tranquility and positivity to the overall ambience of that house. During dinner, she generally played soft instrumental music or old Bollywood songs and that relaxed us after a long tiring day. The interiors had all kinds of lights ranging from dull to bright and the furniture perfectly complemented the overall architecture. We had the best of the crockeries to choose from every day, and my mother felt more than delighted to do it. Mummy always preferred that we speak to each other while eating rather than watching TV or peeping into our devices. She felt that way we could give more quality time to each other. And that did wonders to our interpersonal relations as a family.

Today it was different. At the breakfast table, *bhai* was silently eating and I was lost in my own world. He was oblivious to everything around and I was sitting with my cheek resting on one hand and the other hand just rolling the fork over the noodles. Bhai could make out that I was not in the mood to have breakfast. I knew he too was shattered but I was sure that he'd calmly handle the situation.

He looked at me and said, "Listen, *Gudda*, I know you want me to be around you and papa instead of running behind my work; but it's not about work, it's about commitments that I have made to a lot of people. It's about the completion of this task at hand which my clients owe me.

This Township project is my dream. I have been working head over heels to accomplish this dream of mine. People have put in a lot of effort and money into it. And I cannot put that on stake. It's mandatory to complete this project on time. Apart from the investors and employees, people who've paid for their dream homes are eagerly waiting. Considering that I have to give possession to buyers within a year, I have a lot of work lined up."

Bhai was working on a township project which was to be named Vindur.

"Also, our relatives, friends and neighbours will surely visit our place. Some, to pay sincere condolences and others, just for some extra gossip about mummy's tragic death. So, one of us needs to be there."

He was ready to leave for Chandigarh. Willingly or unwillingly he had to leave, life had to move on, no matter how deep his wounds were.

Sometimes life puts you in a situation where you have to do a lot of things against your will and wish. But one has to accept the harsh reality and make peace with it. Today, we were in that situation.

Bhai brought me closer to hug me. He kissed my forehead saying goodbye. As he began walking towards the door, I could not hold back my tears and started weeping. He turned back to me and hugged me once again.

"Hey, stop crying... Please don't make it difficult for me. You know I can't leave you in tears. It'll make my journey worse than I can imagine. C'mon now... stop crying," he said.

Gasping for breath, I said, "*Bhai*, I don't think I'll be able to do it. I just don't feel confident anymore. I won't be able to take care of daddy. I feel so low already. Please *bhai*, please don't go."

Choking back on his tears he said, "I feel more helpless than I have ever felt. Leaving you in this situation is not at all easy for me and I am sure my thoughts will constantly wander around you and daddy. But you have to be strong, and we as a team have to manage everything."

Daddy's voice from behind interrupted our conversation. He sounded pained and frustrated but at the same time he said,

"Sarth! Bhushan is waiting for you."

Daddy continued, "You are getting late for your flight. Commitments are not meant to be broken. Isn't this what your mother taught you? Then what holds you back here? Go and fulfil your commitments. And you can take Nidhi along. I don't need anyone to look after me."

"No, daddy. I want to stay here with you," I said.

Daddy just nodded.

When *bhai* looked at me, I gave him a subtle nod and said, "Take care and have your food on time."

He left immediately after that. I stood there, motionless.

Now it was only the two of us in Pune. I had to cancel my admission in Chandigarh and admit myself in Pune. I decided to shift here because daddy wanted to stay in Pune. Until when, he didn't know... The reason I shifted here was because my brother had to be in Chandigarh and leaving daddy to suffer alone was out of the question. We'd tried asking him a couple of times in the recent past about returning to Chandigarh. After all, that was our home. Our business was in Chandigarh.

But daddy never answered us.

A few days ago, when daddy asked *bhai* to go back to Chandigarh and look after work, it was apparent that he wasn't keen on joining back, at least, for some more time.

Next morning, I was ready to leave for college. I quickly grabbed a bite from the breakfast table and was about to leave. I waved at him and said bye. My father replied "no"

in an angry tone. I asked him in confusion, "What no Daddy?"

"You are not driving yourself to college, Bhushan will drop you."

"But why? I mean I can go on my own."

Dad was trembling when he spoke; something was bothering him. But what I didn't know.

I asked him politely, "What's wrong daddy?"

"You are going with Bhushan and that's an order."

This was the first time my father had spoken to me in a raised voice.

"But what if I have to go somewhere else from college?" I resisted.

Daddy called Bhushan. "Bhushan..." Louder the second time he called, "Bhushan..."

Bhushan came running and was panting as he spoke. "Yes, *Saab*."

"Drive Nidhi to her college and wait outside till she is done. Take her wherever she wants to go. Don't let her drive alone."

"Okay *Saab*," said Bhushan.

On my way, I couldn't stop thinking of daddy and his weird behaviour. I thought of discussing this with *bhai* post-college.

I reached college.

COEP, the third oldest college in India. A heritage college with a one-of-its-kind architecture. As soon as I entered, I could see curious faces and long stares. It felt like most of them were talking about me. I could see a strange discomfort in the eyes of the girls when they saw me walk around the campus. On the other hand, the boys seemed excited. I finally reached my class. It seemed like the professors already knew about me and my background and so everyone was very warm and welcoming. The professor also introduced me to the class and asked the students to help me with notes and other information until I settle down. During the break, a few of them walked up to me and introduced themselves, just to make me feel comfortable. Two guys shared their contact number and one asked for mine. I took a conscious effort in ignoring the way our class girls behaved with me. I met Sushant, Mahira, Aditi, Kabir and Aman on the first day of my college. Sir had introduced us to each other. Mahira asked me to join them at the canteen. I didn't feel ready to sit around people as yet, but my brother really wanted me to move on. Reluctantly, I joined the group at the canteen. Everybody ordered something to eat. I ordered espresso. My sleepless nights had no end, and my only saviour during the day was coffee. Considering that I was a stranger to all of them, everyone was formal with me. Just to make me feel a part of them, Aditi started talking to me and asked me where I came from.

"Chandigarh," I said.

"So what made you shift to Pune?"

I hesitated a bit and said, "Ahhhh long story! Will tell you some other day."

"Sure. Whenever you are comfortable."

We spoke casually and had a good time. I was missing my old friends. Keeping my fake smile intact was another task at hand. While leaving, I exchanged numbers with a few of them. As soon as I got into the car, I called *bhai*.

"Hey, *Gudda*, how was your first day at college?"

"It was good, but I want to talk to you about something important."

He could sense something fishy and asked what happened.

I told him how daddy had reacted when I was leaving for college.

"Promise me that you won't ask daddy about anything," he said.

"This means you know what is bothering him."

"No, I don't, but I don't want you to bother him either."

"Bother him? I am trying to help."

"No need. Nidhi, please try and understand. You don't have to argue about something which is so sensitive."

"Bhai…"

"No means no, *Gudda*… Bye for now."

The call had ended.

I had tears in my eyes, I was missing mummy. If she would have still been there this wouldn't have happened. I was craving for a hug, I wanted a shoulder to cry on, someone to hold me.

When I was deep in these thoughts Bhushan interrupted me, saying we had reached home.

I wiped my tears while entering home and started humming like always. "I am home," I announced, pretending everything was okay. Daddy didn't even respond. He was sitting on the rocking chair in balcony embracing mom's photo in his arms. I checked with Kamla *kaaki* if dad had eaten anything. She told me he hadn't had anything at all despite *kaaki's* frequent reminders.

I knew convincing daddy to eat was impossible. He just wouldn't agree. But letting daddy sleep hungry was not at all a good idea. So, I whispered something in *kaaki's* ear.

After a while, she went to daddy and said, "*Saab*, baby is refusing to have dinner. Do something, *Saab*."

I was sure daddy will come to me and ask me to eat. And to convince me, it was obvious that he had to eat too. This is exactly what happened. Although this idea worked out, there was a lot that had to be done to ensure daddy's wellbeing. He had lately become absent-minded and was constantly oblivious to everything. And this was all probably because he didn't cry. I didn't see him crying aloud even once after mummy's tragic death. He stayed numb for hours on some days. Daddy's condition started scaring me. I knew I had to do something before it was too late.

What I was doing was completely different from what *bhai* wanted me to do. He wanted me to mingle with people around me in college and our neighbourhood. He wanted me to sleep and eat on time because I had daddy's responsibility too. *Bhai* frequently called up to check on my wellbeing. I knew my condition here would affect his life in Chandigarh. So, I ensured I did well to keep him away from stress.

People at college started thinking of me as absent-minded. They found me dull and boring. Because of my gloomy face, nobody knew the real me who was full of zeal and enthusiasm. My mother's sudden demise had changed everything. But did people's perception of me really matter? For me what mattered at this point in time was my father and *bhai*. All I wanted was a normal life for the three of us. I was tired of crying and grief. I made every attempt to move on. I started sleeping for a little while that I could. I stopped skipping meals, even if it was just a few bites. I made sure I attended college everyday.

But nothing amused me about life anymore.

However, there was one thing that had started catching my attention. It was strange. I felt like I had started feeling deeply for Kabir. There were innumerable times when I found him staring at me. I would constantly find concern, curiosity and love in the way he looked at me. Whenever we were in a group, he paid a little more attention to me than others. He pampered me but was also careful to ensure that his care wasn't vivid. I convinced myself that it was a part of his benevolent personality. But my gut constantly kept on nudging me that he had a special feeling for me.

It was just another day at college. I was sitting in the cafeteria, pondering on how life had changed for the worse. Aditi came to me and interrupted my thoughts.

"Hey, Nidhi!"

"Hi, dear..."

"So, I'm hoping to see you at the cycle rally tomorrow..."

"Cycle rally?"

"We had discussed this almost a week ago and you agreed to attend it, remember?"

"I actually don't."

"Never mind. Tomorrow, we all are joining a cycle rally at 6:30 a.m. and I'm hoping you too are joining us. I'll

WhatsApp you the venue, dress code and our meeting point."

I had to say okay because of the enthusiastic way in which she invited me to join.

I had made up my mind about skipping the rally and college both. Most of my friends would be at the rally so there was no point in going to college alone. After Aditi left, I was again lost in my thoughts and was scribbling on paper with my chin rested on my fist. Kabir came to me and seeing him I was perplexed as to what made him come there. I was amazed to see him approach me because he had never done this before. It was the first time he had come to talk to me. My pale face had turned rosy pink with his presence. My heart was pounding really fast. The pen fell down from my hand. It was really hard for me to keep my emotions in check. He picked up the fallen pen for me. I started the conversation with thank you.

"You are not fine, are you? You have developed dark circles around your eyes."

I was a bit hesitant when I answered because I couldn't tell him in the first meet what I was going through. I thought for a while and said,

"No, I am good, as fit as a fiddle."

He smiled and after a long pause he said, "So you are coming tomorrow, aren't you?"

I certainly said a yes.

"You have a cycle?" He asked.

"Yes, I do."

He left saying, "See you tomorrow then."

For a change I was happy that day, I don't exactly know why and I didn't even want to know. After all, happiness had knocked on my door after so *so* long.

Aditi had messaged me the details. Everyone had to wear a white t-shirt for the rally. The rally was organised to support an eco-friendly environment around the city. The journey was supposed to start at 6:30 a.m. and end by 10:00 a.m. I was excited about the rally, mainly because Kabir was going to be there.

In the morning I reached the venue on time. Bhushan dropped me and my cycle at the venue. My eyes were searching for Kabir. As I reached the venue, I could see many banners advertising the sponsors and many others featuring benefits of cycling. There was a big hoarding at the entrance which read, 'One lac cash prize for the most stylish and fastest cyclist'. The rally was about to begin but I didn't find my friends anywhere. I was feeling anxious and lost in the crowd. I was sure Kabir was with the whole group so I thought of calling Aditi but then I realised I had left my phone in the car. Actually, I had left it deliberately thinking it might disturb me while cycling. But now I was regretting it. Bhushan had already left because I had asked him to leave and come back by 10. I was clueless about how to get in touch with them. I asked a few of our classmates about our group. Finally, one of them said that she had seen them just a minute ago. I turned around to look for them, and just as I turned around, I saw him. I wanted to stand there and keep looking at him forever.

"Gosh! I have been looking for you, where were you?" I asked Kabir.

"I was busy with the photo session."

"Photo session?"

"Nothing important. Let's go and join the rally; it is about to begin."

I just nodded.

The rally began. He was looking so fit and attractive while he was riding. He looked like a macho man. The kind you wouldn't want to mess around with. I was imagining myself in his arms and could not take my eyes off him. My speed was slower than his. He turned back several times to see where I had reached and waited a couple of times for me. When he stood for the third time, I told him not to wait for me and continue the rally at his normal speed. He agreed but still continued looking for me. I was glad but at the same time, it was bothering me as I knew it was affecting his performance in the rally. I loved him around me and secretly enjoyed all the attention he gave me. My attention diverted from him to a fallen tree at the roadside, and he vanished all of a sudden. I thought he must have gone ahead to join the participants who were much ahead as I had asked him not to wait. I was disheartened to be alone once again but I realised that this rally was important for him so it didn't bother me much.

After a while, my speed became slower than it already was, and I soon realised that I was probably the last rider in the rally. Suddenly, I felt very weak and dizzy. I fell down due to the giddiness. And to my surprise I wasn't the last one in the rally, there was someone else behind me. It was Kabir. He had stayed behind just to be with me. I was fortunate he was there because there was no one else around. He parked his cycle and rushed towards me.

My cycle was partially over me when I fell down, he quickly lifted the cycle and kept it aside. He was extremely worried and confused. He sat down and put his hand towel below my head. He asked me if I was fine. I could sense distress in his tone. He gave me his hand for support for me to get up. But I was still feeling weak.

"What's wrong, Nidhi? What happened to you?

You should have stopped immediately when you felt uneasy. Don't you think you should have been more careful?"

I told him I was fine.

"No you are not, you look sick already."

Did you have water before starting? It may be dehydration."

"Forget water I've not had anything since yesterday."

His eyes widened.

"What? But why?"

"Are we continuing this conversation in this position itself?"

"Oh, I am sorry. Try getting up."

I was holding his hand tightly but still could not manage to get up. The time he held my hand was magical. He walked a little ahead to look for a place to sit. There was a restaurant. He lifted me in his arms and made me sit inside and ordered a bottle of water. I was feeling very uncomfortable and weak. I wanted to go home at the earliest. I asked Kabir for his phone.

"Can I use your phone to make a call to my driver? I want to ask Bhushan to pick me up. I have left my phone in the car."

"Of course, you can use my phone. But only after you eat something."

I just gave a small nod and blinked my eyes in acceptance.

The waiter brought a bottle of mineral water and asked for our order. Kabir asked him to come after a while. He poured me a glass of water. After having it, I felt a little better. But I still wanted to go home at the earliest just to gain back my lost energy. So, I asked for his phone again. I guess he wanted to spend some more time with me and didn't want me to make this call now. But he couldn't refuse me for the second time.

"Sure." He said and handed me his phone. My hands were shivering. I could not even hold the cellphone properly and the phone slipped from my hand and broke. I took it back immediately to check if it was working, but to my dismay, it wasn't.

I started apologising.

"I'm so sorry, Kabir! You had to leave your rally in between and now I broke your phone too. I am really sorry!"

"It's okay."

I kept on saying sorry.

He softly pressed my shoulder and said, "It's okay, Nidhi. You are making a big deal out of it. It's just a phone. I will buy a new one. Right now, it's more important that you eat something."

He called the waiter again and asked me for my order.

"Please don't bother, Kabir, I really don't want to have anything."

He frowned at me, an expression that one shows only to a beloved.

I was wondering if he was actually always so kind or if this gesture was especially for me? But then I suddenly realised that I could think about this later too. Right now, it was more important that I order something to eat. I ordered a veg sandwich and asked what all they had in juices.

"Orange, sweet lime, pineapple and Ganga Jamuna," the waiter said.

"Ganga Jamuna?"

"A blend of two fruits."

"Ohh. I'll have orange juice. Kabir, what about you?"

"Tea."

"This is not done, you have to give me company in having breakfast."

He agreed immediately.

"One idli sambar, and yes dip the idlis in sambar, don't bring them separately."

Kabir was watching me with a question mark on his face.

"Do you want me to ask you repeatedly or you are telling me on your own?" he finally asked.

"What?"

"Why haven't you had anything since yesterday?"

"Oh, that…!" I almost gave a deaf ear to his question.

"Yes, that." He stressed the topic.

"Kabir, we'll talk about this later, now I am really hungry and thirsty."

"Okay."

There was silence between us and I kept looking around until our breakfast arrived. It was just another ordinary restaurant with barely any care for hygiene. The staff did not even have a dress code and the tables were manky. I wondered if the food was fit to eat. Kabir could make out from my expressions that I did not like the place.

"I know this place is not upto your standards, but I am sorry we did not have any other choice."

"No... No, don't be sorry, in fact, it was the right decision to come and eat something. Had Daddy seen me in this condition, he wouldn't have appreciated it at all. So it's better I eat something before going home."

The breakfast arrived. He asked me to start.

"Go easy, Nidhi. You haven't had anything since yesterday, if you eat fast you may feel nauseous."

"Yes, you are right," I said.

I started eating. The sandwich was good unlike expected.

"If you don't like it, order something else," he said.

"No no, I'm enjoying it."

"Then have one more."

I grinned and said, "I am not even going to finish this one."

"What? You only eat so much?"

"Yeah, that's my appetite."

"Is it because of your appetite or you deliberately eat less to maintain your figure?"

"Not at all. I like to have frequent small meals." Pushing my plate away, I said I am done.

He finished his meal entirely and then ordered tea for himself.

"Now how do we go back, Kabir?"

He asked the waiter who brought tea, for a phone. The waiter had a smartphone too.

"Don't break this one," he teased me.

I just can't let you go

I smiled at his joke and called Bhushan. After ending the call, I gave his phone back.

"So how long will Bhushan take?"

"He said he is a bit far from here. Will take some time. He didn't anticipate that I would call him early."

"If you don't mind, we can go on my cycle to the venue. We've crossed more than a half rally."

"We don't have any other option either," I said.

I behaved rather reluctant, but I was blushing from within at the thought of sitting so close to him. He asked the restaurant manager to keep my cycle safe over there and told him that my driver will come to collect it.

We walked towards his cycle. He sat on the saddle area and made me sit on the top tube. Before he started, he asked me if I was comfortable.

I said yes. There was hardly any distance between us. I did not want this journey to end.

"Nidhi, at any point if you feel uncomfortable, do let me know."

"Yeah."

He was a complete gentleman. I loved his way of caring and pampering me.

As we reached the venue, a member of the crew who was managing the event came to us and said in a very upsetting tone,

"Where were you? I already asked you to be ahead of all. And look at you, you were behind the one I thought was the last. We had to give away the cash prize to someone else against our wills. You are a cycling champion and who else do you see as stylish as you in the rally? No one! The head of our crew is very upset with me as I was in constant touch with you regarding today's event. I am answerable to the team. They wanted you to win. The winner's photos and videos were supposed to be used in the advertising boards by the main sponsor who is the owner of a big cycle company. We had already selected you for that and it was an unbiased decision as you deserved it. That's why they asked me to complete your photo session as soon as you arrived because they wanted the best of your pics. Now, will you tell me where you were?"

"Yeah, only if you allow me to!" Kabir said in a slightly irritated tone. "My friend had fainted. So, I stood back to help her out." The crew member felt ridiculed. "So was it only you who could help her in the whole rally? There were many more who could help her. You knew this was an important day for you and us." The crew member said.

"I know but I could not find anyone known and I could not rely on any stranger to look after her."

She got pissed off and said, "What's done cannot be undone. We can't do anything to make it better." She left furiously.

For a while, I kept on looking at Kabir and said,

"You were supposed to win one lac rupees, hoardings with your pictures were to be hung all around the city. How could you even think of missing this opportunity? You should have made the most out of it. Opportunities knock but not every time. And this was one of a kind." He was quietly listening and I was feeling very guilty.

"I wish I could reverse it," I said

"But I don't wish to," he said, his eyes full of love for me.

First, the crew member lectured him, now it was the turn of our friends. I saw them coming towards us. Aditi reached us and immediately started rebuking Kabir. He gave her the same explanation that he offered to the crew member. Actually, he didn't mind Aditi scolding him, for she was a very dear friend of his and at the same time she was a gem of a person. Actually, Kabir wanted to escape this conversation as he had no valid reason for not having participated in the rally. Hence, when she started firing him, he just said, "I have something important to do, I'll leave now. Please excuse me!" And then he left.

Aditi was disheartened, she had so much to vent out. As soon as Kabir had left she started talking about it to me.

"Nidhi, Kabir seldom does anything so insane. He is very smart and sensible. I can say I've never seen a person with so much maturity and patience. He's a perfect blend of wisdom, good looks and high moral values. I wonder why he did something so stupid. He could have called me to help you out. I would have done it with equal happiness and sincerity. And I being in the rally wasn't as important as much as Kabir's presence was. Moreover, one lac rupees means a lot to him. Nevertheless, there is no point in crying over spilt milk."

Bhushan reached the spot where he had dropped me. We were talking while walking towards the exit gate. As Aditi noticed him arrive, she said, "Okay then see you and take care. Get well soon."

"Bye Aditi, see you."

I left for home.

All the way and even after reaching I was just thinking of him. Why did he do it? To impress me or to genuinely be around me? But if so, he could have spent time with me some other time. I was going nowhere. Why did he sacrifice one lac rupees for the little time we spent together? I was really confused. Why did he miss out on such a great opportunity? A part of my heart was really happy that he did this for me but the other half was really sad that he lost the money and a great opportunity because of me. That day was a little different from the past few days. I kept thinking of him all day long, and barely slept at night. I was either falling in love or I was already into it, couldn't understand.

Next morning when I reached college there were only few students in the class. I wondered how so many students were absent on the same day. To my delight Kabir was present. I wildly guessed that it might be a mutual bunk by all friends and I was right. Kabir told me that all of them had taken a common off as most of them were exhausted due to the previous day's cycle rally. He added these few are the studious ones who don't understand the language of fun and unity hence they had come.

"So, are you among the studious ones?"

He smiled and said, "They had messaged in our Whatsapp group about the common off but since my phone broke yesterday, I didn't get to know about this. And I guess you are not yet added in the group hence you too didn't know about this either."

"Oh... So what's the point of sitting in class, I guess we should go back then."

I wanted him to stop me, and ask me out for a coffee or a walk in the park.

"Nidhi…"

"Yes, Kabir…"

"Did you have your breakfast today?"

"No… ."

"So, if you don't have anything important to do, can we… can we go and have something to eat somewhere out of college?"

Instead of hitting him with an instant yes, I acted as if was not sure if I wanted to go, and finally said, "Okay, let's go."

"Do you like Chinese?" he asked.

"Yes, I love Chinese."

"There's a new Chinese restaurant nearby, we can go there."

"Sure."

While we were walking towards the parking, he told me that after reaching college he called Aditi and that's when he got to know about common off. I just nodded.

"Kabir, your phone is in a very bad state and I guess it will barely get repaired. Please allow me to buy you a new one."

"Don't bother, I've already ordered a new one. I had taken it for repair yesterday itself and you are right. He said the same, it is of no use now, it's not repairable."

"Kabir, please don't get me wrong, I am not bragging about my wealth or trying to show off, but it's a very small amount for me to spend, so please allow me to buy you the phone. Anyway, it's my fault so I owe you one. Please. Please it is a request, else I'll keep feeling guilty."

"Okay… Okay, you may."

"You cancel the order you've placed. So, shall it be my choice or yours?"

"Yours."

I grinned.

He grinned back.

We reached his bike, he sat and lifted his bike's stand, wore his helmet and offered me one too. It was a clear indication that he wanted me to come with him on his bike but for now, I decided to keep the distance unless I was sure. Although I knew he was the right person, I was answerable to my family. I said I'll follow him.

We reached the restaurant and unlike the previous day, this restaurant's ambience was too good. There were very few people at the restaurant as it was afternoon time and that too on a weekday. He chose a table at a corner. He pulled the chair for me. We ordered schezwan noodles. He could not take his eyes off me, and the very moment I noticed him staring at me, he pretended to be watching elsewhere.

"Shall I ask you something?"

"Yes, sure."

"Yesterday you could have asked someone else to help me and could have continued the rally, then why did you choose to be there yourself?"

He was quiet.

"You don't want to answer?"

"I want to but…"

"But…?"

"Just not sure how to begin."

"No worries... go on..."

"Okay... I have a confession to make. I had seen you in Pune two years back and that too not for very long, just a glance in a mall. I had even followed you for a while, obviously, you did not notice it.

You know there was a blurred image of a girl in my mind whom I would love, with whom I'll spend my life. I often dreamt of the girl in the image. But after I saw you that vague image had become clear. I never saw you after that. When it was your first day in college, I was over the moon. I don't know what it is. Even yesterday what I could see was only you. There was nothing else I remembered."

Although Kabir was very sharp and witty, there was an innocence in him which I could see. Which left me no option but to believe in him.

I was speechless.

The noodles had arrived and the presence of the waiter distracted both of us.

None of us spoke about it after that. Later, while leaving I asked him his address so that I could send him his new phone at the earliest.

Of the friends I made in college, I found Aditi very understanding and mature. She was very helpful. Even though Kabir was a great help too, but I preferred Aditi in many places over Kabir. Aditi was a better option for me since she was less distracting. I gave her a call.

"Hey, Aditi, Nidhi here."

"Oh! Hi Nidhi. How are you doing?"

"I am good. Actually, I wanted to know if you can meet me for a while. I'd like to talk to you about something important."

"I will be glad to help you."

"Okay! So, shall I pick you up now?"

She agreed and gave her address. I reached her home within 20 minutes, and Bhushan came along as usual. As she entered the car, I told her that I wanted to visit some psychiatrist. Aditi was dumbfounded. Before she asked me for further details, I started telling her everything that I was going through. She barely knew anything about me and now that she was here to help me, she had to know everything to be able to help me. And I myself wanted to share it with someone. I was tired of keeping my feelings to myself.

"That day you were asking me about the reason for shifting here. We had to shift here due to the sudden demise of my mother. I'm not disturbed because we shifted here, I'm just not able to get over my mother's tragic death."

"What happened to your mom? And what exactly made you shift to Pune from Chandigarh?" Aditi asked.

"My brother and I received a call from Daddy telling us about mom's sudden death. Pune is actually my mom's hometown. She had a deep emotional connection with the city. She was an orphan but was always strong from within. She was determined to build her own old age home and orphanage. Mummy always spent everything she had for those orphans and the old residents at her home. When my parents got married, my father gave her all the happiness in the world that a husband could. But she missed her city and Vindur always."

"Vindur?"

"She had named her orphanage home as Vindur."

Aditi was listening to me with complete sincerity and concern.

"Mom came to Pune in almost every 6 months, and after we were born, she brought us too.

But my father didn't like my mother staying at a home with orphans and with no luxuries. My father had worked very hard to reach where he is today. He always wanted to offer every possible luxury to my mother.

Although she declined a new house in Pune, Daddy gifted her one. It was built exactly the way she wished her house to be. Right from curtains, to the colour of walls, the interiors, the choice of flowers and plants in the garden, everything was the way mummy liked them to be. It is full of positive vibrations and one of its kind. When we were kids, we came here during vacations. Later when we grew up, we came whenever we wished to. This time my parents had come to spend some time with each other. They loved being around each other." I said with a smile, with my eyes filled with tears.

"They had been married for the last 27 years but the spark between them was as fresh as new. Every time mummy and Daddy went to Pune, *bhai* and I received a call after a few days to come down to Pune and be with them. But this time the call we received from Daddy shattered the two of us.

A few days back we had asked Daddy to come back with us but he didn't agree. I never said that I want to stay here. In fact, I wanted the three of us to go back, but *bhai* knew this was not the correct time to force Daddy to come back. So, it was understood that I'd stay back with Daddy. *Bhai* is a wise man and so are his decisions. I did not argue and decided to stick to the plan."

"So, what does your brother do?"

"He is working on a township project. My Daddy and my brother, are both engineers."

"Which college did you study at in Chandigarh?"

"CCETC (Chandigarh College of Engineering and Technology). I loved going to college although I am not very passionate about engineering, but I loved it because I had my friends there. When *bhai* asked me to complete my last year of engineering here in Pune, I resisted, mainly because I knew I wouldn't find such friends elsewhere. Eventually, I had no option but to agree."

"You always wanted to be an engineer?"

"I have never even given a thought on what exactly I wanted to pursue. I just went with the flow and this subject came along. And unlike other students, I am not even conscious about my grades, career in general."

"Why?"

"Maybe because I have had everything, always. We were always raised with a golden spoon throughout. I always got whatever I asked for. We were not just conferred with a good lifestyle, but our parents made it a point to give us unbudgeted time and love as well. Besides I got lucky by having my mom's genes, mainly because of the way she looked."

Aditi interrupted me saying, "Yes, Nidhi, you are really beautiful. You are a beauty with brains. I have never seen someone as beautiful and rich at the same time."

"Aditi, you are so generous with your words. Means a lot to me. Thank you so much! You are really good at making people feel good about themselves."

"C'mon, Nidhi. I am being honest. Anyway, I'd like to know more about your mother."

"I was always content in having a mother who had a solution to everything. Mummy knew me more than I knew myself, not only me, this was the case with *bhai* and Daddy too. Although *bhai* is very wise and capable of doing almost everything on his own, but even then he liked to rely on mummy for certain things. Daddy and I on the contrary, are not capable of taking care of ourselves. We always needed someone to take care of us emotionally. Mummy was that person for the two of us. Daddy was extremely dependent on mummy for everything. This is the reason he is shattered now. Mummy was the lifeblood, the vital spark and the soul of our family. The wounds in our hearts of losing our soulmate are growing deeper day-by-day. Being the youngest one at home I have always been pampered by all three of them. Unfortunately, now only by two of them.

About coming here, I feel maybe because I was content, I did not have any goal or ambition in life. I never took my decisions on my own so when *bhai* decided that I should complete my last year of civil engineering over here in Pune, I did not object."

"So COEP was your brother's decision?"

"Yes. *bhai* decided to take my admission in COEP. He asked me if I had a say about the choice of college because he did not want to impose his decision on me, he wanted my consent. *Bhai* was, in fact, asking me if I needed a bodyguard."

Aditi's jaw dropped listening to this. "Bodyguard! But why?"

"My reaction was the same when *bhai* asked me. He explained saying that we have not grown up here so we are not familiar with this city. It feels like home in Chandigarh. But everything over here is very new. He was worried if it was safe or not. Everyone's intentions are not clean. Some may think of taking advantage. *Bhai* still treats me like a little one. He constantly feels the need to protect me. I have always seen a protective and pampering environment around me. Oh, by the way, Aditi, I just realised I haven't stopped talking for a while now. I've been so preoccupied with my talks that I forgot you might be getting late."

"Oh, come on. On the contrary, I am glad you trusted me with your secrets and opened up before me."

I then told her the reason for visiting a psychiatrist. We googled the list of psychiatrists. We scrutinised the list for the doctors with the best reviews and ratings. We shortlisted one and decided to visit her. Dr. Arundhati Goel who was a very renowned and experienced doctor. Aditi told me about her while on our way and it was evident with the way Dr. Arundhati spoke to us. She was a sharp-witted lady. The astute doctor was able to quickly assess Daddy's situation. After a long conversation in which I told her Daddy's situation, she asked me one question which I could not answer. The question which shook me.

"What exactly happened to your mom? What were her last words to your Daddy?" She wanted me to answer this before going ahead and I could understand that she had to uncover all facts to give the right treatment to Daddy. I would have definitely answered it if I knew it all.

I left saying, "I'll revert to you very soon, thank you."

I was frustrated when I came out of the clinic. Aditi understood and hence did not ask me anything further. From the conversation that I had with Dr. Goel, the picture was very clear and she understood that keeping quiet at the moment would be better. She said, "Don't worry, Nidhi. There'll definitely be some way out, and I am sure we'll soon figure it out." I hugged her showing my gratitude towards her. I dropped her back home.

As I entered home, the first thing I checked on was Daddy; he was fast asleep. I immediately rushed to my room and called *bhai*. He answered, "How are you *Gudda*, how is Daddy?"

"What do you think I am to you?" I asked him but was not looking for an answer. I was weeping, "Why are you doing this to me? Don't I have the right to know what happened to my own mom? This ambiguity is bothering me like hell. I can't take it anymore. Why don't you tell me what happened to our mother?"

Bhai realised that I was not letting him leave me unanswered. He had tried to avoid this situation for so many days.

"*Gudda*, please calm down."

"Don't calm me. This time I want an answer, not an excuse."

"*Gudda*, I can't tell you. Please try to understand."

"What should I understand?"

"I don't want your state to be like Daddy's. Just put yourself in my shoes and see, we are not able to bring Daddy out of it, and if you too loose control, were will I go? Irrespective of how strong I am, eventually, I am a human being and I have emotions too. Even I feel hurt, just because I don't show it much doesn't mean my sentiments are dead or inactive. Whatever happened to mom, the fact is, she has passed away, she is not with us anymore. She has left the three of us, never to return."

I cried out loud listening to these words. Even *bhai* was crying. He tried to hide it but I could make out. I stopped crying abruptly.

"Okay, *bhai*, I won't ask you again, but yes I will wait for the day when you'll feel I've become strong enough to face the truth."

"*Gudda*, I am sorry."

"No, *bhai*, I completely understand."

"Take care and meet me soon, bye."

"Bye princess, take care."

Next morning when I woke up, I received a call from Aditi. She asked me with genuine concern, 'How are you dear?'

"I am good Aditi, thank you."

"I don't know if I should be asking this or not, because on one side I realise you are down and you need your own space and on the other side, I feel you should go out and relive your life. That way you can first heal your wounds and only then your Daddy's."

"What's the matter? What exactly are you talking about?" I asked her.

"Mahira has invited all of us for her birthday party, and I would be happy if you come along too."

I saw a "call waiting" notification, and it was *bhai*. I told the same to her and told her that I will call her back.

Bhai had just called to check if I was fine. He asked me whom I was talking to. I told him the whole thing. *Bhai* said, "I want you to go, *Gudda*."

"But *bhai*..."

"No, Nidhi, you have to move on someday or the other. And the sooner you move on, the better it will be for all of us."

Mahira had invited all her friends for her birthday party. Not only the close ones but also the casual ones. Everyone who was invited to the party was very excited because a grand party was expected. Mahira was a rich chic and she loved showing off her father's wealth. Her wealthy father and her overall upbringing, was the major cause of her snobbish and spendthrift behaviour. She always spoke about herself and loved being the centre of attention. Whenever the attention moved to someone else, it would offend Mahira. She had an extremely strong need to look good. She had many friends but most of them were with her only because of her money. She always carried a 'my way is the only way' attitude.

It was Saturday evening; the party was at Mi-a-mi J.W Marriott. As usual, Bhushan dropped me to the venue. I asked him to go back after he dropped me, and informed him that my friends were going to drop me back home. He immediately called Daddy and told him exactly what I had said. I started the countdown; I was sure Daddy will call me. 10...9...8...7...6...5...4... and my phone rang. It was Daddy, as expected. Before he spoke, I started speaking.

"Daddy, please stop being so overprotective. I know you are worried, but I'll be very late and my friends will drop me home. Besides, I don't like making Bhushan wait for so long. Please Daddy, I promise if I sense anything wrong, I'll immediately call you."

"Okay *Gudda*, take care... Love you. And be careful."

"Love you too, Daddy... Bye."

"Bye, *Gudda*."

I entered Mi-a-mi. I had heard a lot about this place and the ambience there was exactly the way I had heard about it. Beautiful beyond words. But the place was extremely overpopulated for its size, I guess because of that Kabir was constantly moving around me. He was either being protective or possessive, but I was blushing because of the attention he gave me. I was loving this attention. The interior of the club was out of the world and the dance floor too. It was a very decent place to hang out. The DJ was a well-known artist and music too was apt.

Kabir was looking very appealing. I had my eyes on him throughout the evening and as he was being so protective, that attracted me even more towards him. He was wearing deep blue jeans, a plain black t-shirt and a grey jacket. I was wearing a simple knee-length, off-shoulder, black dress and I had left my hair open. We both were so engaged in each other's company, that I didn't even notice that I'd finished three cocktails. Although they were soft cocktails, because of so many drinks, I could feel my bladders bursting. I rushed to the restroom. When I was inside the toilet, I heard Mahira and Aditi talking. Mahira was no less than a bitch, in exact words.

"Listen, Aditi, I have a plan for Kabir and me."

"What plan?" Aditi replied to her.

"First of all, I will ask him to dance, which I am sure he won't refuse. I'll make sure that I booze so much that I start stumbling and when I'll be in an unconscious state, a strong man like him will ensure that he drops me home safely. And here look at this," she said pointing at her cleavge, "my... he won't be able to focus on anything else once he sees this so close to him. My touch will stimulate him instantly. It will give him a sensual feeling like never before."

"Mahira you are sounding so desperate to sleep with him," Aditi spoke in astonishment.

"What do you mean, of course, I am desperate to make love to him."

"I thought you liked him, I thought you genuinely loved him." Aditi said in a hesitant tone.

"You are such a moron, Aditi! Why would I do all this if I didn't like him? You have seen the efforts I have taken to get him close to me. You know how he is, he doesn't take a quick interest in every girl and every proposal. And I can't force him to love me. But this surely is a great chance."

After this conversation, they left the washroom but I was still inside thinking of everything that I heard. I was in a state of shock. Girls being attracted to Kabir was obvious. He was after all, very handsome. His exceptionally lean and toned body, shredded abs made him look hotter than many boys around him. He had the kind of personality that could woo almost every woman effortlessly.

When I heard Mahira talking about making love to him, even my thoughts were wandering around being in bed with him. I never thought on these lines before.

I got up with a twitch and rushed out immediately. I was searching for Kabir on the floor. I found him dancing with Mahira.

I did not have any clue about what I was going to do next. I never felt this way for anyone else. I was wondering why it bothered me. Afterall, Kabir and I were not even committed, but it somehow made me very jealous. I suddenly felt possessive about him.

I didn't give it a second thought and dragged him furiously out of the bar saying, "I need to talk, come out with me." He quickly agreed, so that saved any extra efforts from my end. I could see a big question mark on his face. He was quiet. He could sense my uneasiness. I started speaking quickly and loudly. "Kabir, Mahira and her intentions are not pure. She wants to sleep with you despite knowing that you are not ready for it. She was trying to instigate you with her actions today. I brought you here to make you alert."

In a bewildered expression, Kabir said, "Make me alert?"

Then I said, "I mean trying to save you."

"So, you think if she tried to arouse me, I would have done what she wanted?"

I was confused when I spoke, "I don't know. I don't think you would have done it, but I hardly know you. Besides, any normal boy would fall prey to her intentions. She may have successfully attracted you towards her."

His unmoving gaze made it more difficult for me to choose my words.

"Whether we sleep together or not, how does that matter to you?"

I was avoiding this question because I did not have an answer to this, I was embarrassed. I started walking away, without saying anything. After I walked a few steps, I was expecting him to call me. Although I couldn't understand why I expected so much out of him, I hardly knew him, he hardly knew me, why so many expectations then? My thoughts were interrupted by his voice.

"Nidhi wait…"

I took a sigh of relief and immediately stopped. He came to me.

"I can see that you feel something for me and so do I; it's too early to name it as love, but it's surely something special. And I am sure whatever you did this evening was out of that special feeling which I guess you haven't yet figured out."

He was so correct. I was astonished. He was so precise.

I asked him, sounding like a kid, "How did you know this?"

He just hugged me and said, "Come, let's go inside."

He held my hand to take me in. A shiver ran through my body as he touched me and I felt lost in his world.

"Come, Nidhi…"

Resisting to go inside, I held his hand with my other one.

In a very humble tone he said, "Nidhi, we are here for her birthday party and I was dancing with her, and you brought me here abruptly, it doesn't look good. Please, let's go inside."

"I'll come inside but I don't want to stay here for long."

He gave me a comforting nod.

As we got in, he apologised to Mahira and told Aditi that he wanted to go home as it was too late.

He came closer to my ear and asked, "Do you want me to drop you or Aditi?" I pressed my index finger a little over his abs signing that I wanted him to drop me. He then waved to all and said, "You guys carry on, I'll drop her home." Mahira asked him to take her car and drop me, which would ensure that he came back there.

Mahira was already annoyed as her plan didn't work out so she tried another throw of a dice. It did bother me, but I had something else going on in my mind at that time. We didn't speak till we reached the car, he opened the door for me. There were many thoughts strolling around my mind. I was tickled pink with whatever had happened.

He seemed normal, but I wanted to break the silence between us. Until I could think of something to speak, he said, "Where to Nidhi? I mean where do you stay?"

Of everything else under the sun, he asked me this silly question.

With great disappointment, I told him my address.

"Will someone be waiting for you at home?"

"Yes, Daddy must be awake."

"Okay"

"Are you still upset about what has happened?'

"Not at all."

Again, silence engulfed us. We reached home.

He asked me in a concerned tone, "Do u want me to drop you inside or you'll go on your own?"

I wanted to invite him inside; I didn't want him to go. Although we didn't even have a word when we were together in the car, I still wanted him to come inside. But again, I was not sure how Daddy must be, or what he was up to. After mummy's death, Daddy had become unpredictable. "I'll go by myself," I said.

"Thank you, Kabir. Goodnight."

He wished me goodnight and left.

I turned around to leave when he called my name.

I had a big smile on my face and my eyes shone bright, I turned around hiding my expressions.

"You look very pretty today." He said in a sensuous voice.

I was dancing in my mind.

He said bye after a few seconds and left.

Later while walking towards the house, I realised, I was so overwhelmed with his compliment that I didn't even reply back to him. I went inside swinging but what I saw abashed me. As I entered Kamla *Kaaki* was pacing up and down the living room, she looked very tensed and worried.

"What's wrong, *kaaki*?"

"Baby, I can't find *Saab* anywhere," she said nervously.

I yelled at her, "Can't find? Tell me exactly what has happened!"

"After you left, I asked him for dinner thrice, but *Saab* refused and the fourth time when I asked, *Saab* asked me to leave him alone for the time being. After that, I went to my room and sat on the chair and didn't realise that I dozed off. I woke up and rushed to *Saab's* room to again ask for dinner but he wasn't there."

The next morning when I went to college, I was very tense but at the same time was feeling delighted to see Kabir. The moment he smiled at me, the whole world around me vanished from my sight and all I could see was only him.

During the break I was sitting alone, Kabir came to me and he asked with genuine concern, "What's wrong, Nidhi?"

"How did you guess something is wrong?"

"It isn't a guess, I can see it in your eyes."

I felt as if he had known me for ages.

I took a big pause, he asked me again and then I replied,

"Will you take me somewhere? I need fresh air; I feel cramped over here." He just gave me a nod. He immediately got up and said, "Come, let's go."

As we were heading towards the parking, he asked me, "I have a bike. Will you prefer going out with me on my bike or...?"

He had a Royal Enfield. Although I'd love sitting with him on his bike, this was not the correct time.

I interrupted him. "No, we will go in my car." Bhushan had dozed off in the car. I gave a gentle knock on the door. He woke up, came out of the car and said, "Give me a minute, I'll wash my face and take you where you want."

"No, I have three more friends to pick on my way, so there won't be enough space if you come. We'll be having lunch outside and then have to visit a friend's place. After that, I'll be back home. So, you better take some transport and go home."

"Okay, Nidhi *beta.*"

Kabir could make out that I was not in a condition to drive. He put his hand to ask for the key and said, "I'll drive." I handed him the key and quietly sat beside him.

I was in deep thoughts and was very sad, almost ready to cry anytime.

I just can't let you go

"What is making you cry? I mean what's wrong? I am sorry I have no idea how to deal with girls, which is making it difficult for me to come up with the right words. Please tell me what is bothering you so much."

After a long pause, I spoke.

"Kabir, Daddy is in deep pain and still in a state of shock. It's been more than three weeks since he's been skipping meals, does not sleep properly, sits in a single place for hours. Last night after you dropped me home, our caretaker told me that Daddy was nowhere to be found. After looking for him all around, we found him in the pool. He was there in the pool for four hours at a stretch."

Kabir's eyes widened listening to this.

"I kept on asking Daddy why he got inside the pool during the night time. He was numb. We brought him out after great efforts. He didn't even change and just dozed off. We pleaded with him to at least change his clothes and have something before sleeping, but he did not agree. My father's situation is killing me from inside and my brother is not here either. I'm confused about how to handle Daddy and bring him back to normal. I was raised like a princess, the little one in the family. I have never handled any stress. It was always done by my parents and bhai. But now it's all on me, how do I do this? I really don't know how to deal with this situation."

"What about your mom? Where is she?"

I started crying before answering him. I was not even able to talk. Before I could hold myself and speak, something awful happened which agitated the two of us. We were at a remote place and people hardly commuted through that route. Kabir was on the driving seat but he was not facing the front. He was sitting in a slanting position facing towards me, and

I was facing him. Suddenly, a man with a hockey stick hit the window glass on my side, which broke the glass into pieces. I could not see him doing this because I was facing Kabir, but he saw it just before it happened. As Kabir saw the man hitting the glass he pulled me towards him, hiding me in his arms. Because of his quick action, I was saved from any harm that the man, the hockey stick or the window glass could have caused me. I was petrified. I had clenched Kabir's shirt out of fear. That man tried to reach my arm and wanted to pull me out of the car. Kabir brought me a little closer to him, although there was hardly any space between us. Kabir shouted at the man and looked at him with wide angry eyes. "Dare you touch her; I am warning you." Despite a couple of warnings, the man did not go away. He slowly pushed me away from his arms, and tightly held my shoulder and said, "Just be calm, don't worry, I'll screw him." His eyes were red in anger when he spoke. Kabir got out of the car and had lost control. Just before he could hit the man angrily, two men rushed in there saying, "No sir, please wait, spare him. He is mentally disturbed. Ever since his wife has left him, he finds his wife in every other girl and misbehaves. He is not guilty. Please sir, please forgive him."

Kabir looked at them and said, "Okay, take him away."

While leaving, one of the men who rescued the culprit folded his hands and apologised to Kabir. He said, "I am sorry for the expense you'll have to incur for repairing the window."

"It's okay, you please take care of him and be with him to avoid anything major that he may commit against the innocent," Kabir spoke in a low volume, but his hands were still shivering from the mounting tension.

"Yes, sir, thank you." The three men left the place.

Kabir asked me to come out and be seated at the back.

I just can't let you go

I quietly obeyed.

He picked up the broken glass pieces and threw them away.

"Wait, I'll come and help," I said.

"No way, just relax and sit. The broken pieces may hurt you. I'll do it, you just relax for a bit."

I was continuously staring at him in admiration. I am sure he noticed it, but he did not react and continued doing what he was doing.

"Ummm! No... It's difficult to do it manually, it will only be clean after you give it for servicing, and this car will make you pay a lot this time," he said in a kiddish tone.

I was so lost in him that I barely heard what he said.

He looked at me for my reply. I was blankly staring at him.

"Madam, do you mind sitting at the back or you want me to clear the seat right away so you can sit beside me?"

"Clear it!" I said spontaneously because I knew I wanted to sit as close to him as I could.

After he cleared the seat, he forwarded his hand towards me to come out of the car.

Some current passed through me when I touched his hand. It felt like a magical touch.

"Nidhi, do you have any cushion or jacket or anything else to put on the seat before you sit? Because there are chances a few particles may still be there. So better be safe."

I thought for a few seconds.

"*Na*, nothing in the car. Will this stole do?" I said removing the one I was wearing.

"Will do."

His attention immediately drove to my neck as I removed the stole. I was wearing a deep neck floral top. Till I was wearing a stole it wasn't looking so attractive, but the moment I removed the stole, I guess he went crazy. It was evident from his expressions.

But he instantly diverted his eyes elsewhere to ensure that I don't feel conscious. He then spread the stole on my seat.

"Done."

I was back to my seat.

"Nidhi, you are okay, right?"

I threw myself on him and hugged him. He took a few seconds to hug me back. But the moment he hugged me, I felt there couldn't be any better place in the world. We both got close and our lips met. We kissed each other passionately. I don't know about him, but this was my first kiss. After I realised what was actually happening, I abruptly withdrew and released my lips from his. It was a little embarrassing for both of us. Not because we kissed but because we were not in a relationship as yet. We wanted to avoid talking about it. Kabir very effortlessly started a conversation and made me feel at ease. He asked me, "We were talking about your mom. Where is she?"

I avoided making eye contact, and said in a low voice, "She passed away. When someone so close to heart passes away this is what happens. Like the man we just encountered, has become mentally disturbed. It actually disturbs everything, Kabir. It makes living hell. Their memories kill you every moment. You don't find life worth living anymore. My Daddy is in depression. I always try to console him. I keep counselling him to move on and forget mummy. What is gone is gone. But he just doesn't seem to understand. I have bitten off more than I can chew to bring Daddy out of this.

But he is not ready to forget mom. I know it's very difficult but somehow, we have to bring Daddy out of this. If he continues to live like this, I mean skipping meals, not taking proper rest, not socialising, not sharing his pain, he will soon fall ill. Even *bhai* and I miss mom. *Bhai* is practical which has helped him come out of it, but Daddy... How should we help him?"

Kabir was sincerely listening to me and was waiting for me to finish.

"Say something..."

"Nidhi why do you want Daddy to forget your mom? You are actually working in a wrong direction sweetie. See in life many such things happen which leave us in agony. Some wrong decisions, some misfortunes, some relations which are destined to be the way they are, a sudden demise of the one you live for. But then we have to move on. Life goes on, it doesn't wait for anyone. So instead of sitting and thinking of the past, we should try to improve our future. Your Dad won't ever forget your mom and he actually should not even do that. Let him live for her, like her, in fact he should live two lives at a time, his and hers too. He has to complete her incomplete wishes as he loved her. He has to love you both like a father and a mother at the same time. He has to do those things which she would have done instead. He has to live to make her happy, wherever she is, cherish her love. This is what I feel."

I was amazed with Kabir's thoughts because he saw the same situation in a very different light. His thoughts were very positive. I could see a ray of hope after listening to him.

"Kabir will you help me when I need you?"

He said, "Undoubtedly." I was impressed by his kind and forever-ready-to-help attitude.

"Nidhi it's getting late, let's go."

I gave him a nod. There was some magic in him which took me to oblivion whenever I thought of him. He called out my name twice but I didn't respond until he called it out loud and long for the third time.

"Yes Kabir."

"My bike is in college parking. Will you be able to drive back home alone or you want me to drop you?"

I could have easily driven back home myself, but I said no.

"Will you please drop me home?"

I enjoyed having him around me. Although we spoke less, I still wanted him around me. There were times when unconsciously, I found reasons to be around him.

First, I thought I'll ask my driver to drop him home, but then I thought of something else. When we reached home and got out of the car, I was just trying to frame my words properly so that he wouldn't misunderstand me. Actually, I was a bit nervous, in fact a lot nervous. Before I could complete framing the sentence and speak it out, he said, "I'll take your leave."

"How do you think you'll go?"

"I'll take a cab."

"No, no. You are not going by a cab."

Meanwhile, Bhushan came and said, "Shall I drop your friend?"

I said, "No *kaaka*, no need."

Kabir was a bit confused with my weird behaviour.

"Nidhi, he should not drop me home, I should not go by cab, and I've forgotten my Spider-Man suit at home, because of which I can't even go by climbing walls. How will I go then?" I chuckled at his Spider-Man joke. And he was just smiling. He started moving, and said, "I'll leave B-bye."

I stopped him by holding his hand.

"Take my car along with you and pick me up in the morning."

After I said it, I realised, I was such a moron, I wasted so much time framing it and what did I offer him? A statement, more like an order. How stupid of me.

He was astonished with what I said, but he agreed. I guess he was smart enough to understand, I wanted to be with him or maybe he agreed because he himself wanted to be with me. That night I finished my dinner quickly and started hunting for what I would wear the next morning. Although I knew most of my clothes looked good on me, I was still conscious about what I would wear. After four hours of searching for something suitable and innumerable trials, 80% of the wardrobe was on bed and I was finally done with the selection. I moved all the dresses to a side creating a big lump of clothes, ruining their ironed stiffness, and placed the dress which I had to wear in the centre of the bed. I had kept the pair of bellies ready, matching accessories were also out of their drawers. I was done but didn't feel like sleeping. It was too late and I knew if I slept, I wouldn't wake up. I made myself coffee which was my favourite thing to do. Then I opened his Facebook account and started looking at his pictures. Day-by-day I was losing myself in his world. I was eagerly waiting for the next day. Next morning I got ready much earlier than usual. My tummy was so occupied with dancing butterflies, that it didn't feel like eating anything before leaving home. I was just waiting for his call with my eyes constantly glued to the phone. The phone rang. I smiled from ear to ear.

"About to reach your home." He said.

I came out of the house and sat on the swing in our garden. After many days my thoughts had shifted from the grief of mom's death to the freshness of newly sowed seeds of love. Did I love him? Or was it just infatuation. I didn't know and I didn't even want to know for the time being. I just knew that I wanted him near me. When I was thinking of all this, he arrived. That dusk pale sunlight of the morning, fragrance of our garden, his arrival, it was all so beautiful. I couldn't have asked for anything better. He opened the car door for me like a gentleman. I expected a compliment from him. If not for my looks, at least for the sake of a sleepless night which I spent getting ready for him. But I guess I failed. He didn't utter a word about how I looked. I was hoping he'd praise me. I thought maybe he was too shy to compliment. "Doesn't he like me? Or is it that he hasn't paid heed to my dress so far…?" aaaa…my head will burst.. 'Stop it Nidhi,' a voice from within said. I don't know why he spoke less when we met when there was actually so much to talk about.

The Romeo in him rose when I was getting off the car.

"Nidhi please spare boys."

"What?"

"If you look so gorgeous, how will they pay attention to their studies? Leave studies, how will they pay attention to anything else?"

I stopped and didn't know how to react.

"Nidhi it was a compliment, hope you didn't mind."

I just smiled.

"C'mon let's go," he said.

I went with him as if we were iron and magnet. But then like a blot on the moon, Mahira caught a glimpse of us walking together and her anger knew no bounds. She came to us directly, I wasn't afraid of her but I separated my hand from his.

"Why haven't you come on your bike today?" She asked him with her snobbish attitude.

"It was here in the college parking." Kabir calmly replied.

"Why did you leave it here?"

"Long story, let's go," He said, trying to end the conversation.

Mahira didn't even greet me with a hello, I didn't mind either. She held Kabir's hand and started walking ahead. I was slowly walking behind the two. I was upset with her sudden appearance and the way she reacted. But was relaxed when Kabir slowed down so he could walk beside me. We walked to the class.

I was not at all attentive in the class. I was just waiting for the break so I could talk to him. But he was surrounded by friends during the break. I couldn't ask him to excuse them and come with me. After college he came to me.

"Yes Nidhi, during the break I could not skip the group to be with you."

How did he always manage to read my mind? I wondered.

"How's Daddy?"

"He is as he was." I said without any expression.

"Tell me one thing, what or whom did your mom love the most apart from you three?" he asked.

"It was her home 'Vindur'. She visited it almost daily when she was here in Pune. And frankly speaking, Vindur was the only reason we came here so often."

"Can we visit her home now?"

"Now?"

"Yes, if it's convenient for you."

"Sure, let's go."

Kabir was amazed to see that home. It was nothing extraordinary, but the culture mummy had maintained there was commendable. She actually wanted to devote all her life caring for people in need, but then she fell in love with Daddy. Even after getting married nothing deterred her spirit. She was full of humanity and generosity. Mummy was the reason behind so many smiles. She was the reason why so many stopped crying anymore.

After visiting Vindur, Kabir came to drop me home.

"Kabir I would love it if you came inside."

He was quiet, didn't agree at once. On insisting, he agreed.

Kamla *kaaki* opened the door for us, and enquired at the entry, "your friend?"

"Yes *kaaki*, he is my college friend, Kabir." Our home was a very big and luxurious one. But Kabir did not pay any heed to it. He was a man of honour. Although he must not have seen a lot of such homes earlier, he didn't utter a word about the place unlike those guests who couldn't stop themselves from praising our home.

Kaaki welcomed Kabir with an elderly smile. "Come, come, be seated. It's too hot out there, I'll get you both some masala lemonade."

This was my daily summer routine, having a lemonade after I came back home. But since different people have different tastes and preferences, I asked Kabir if he was okay with lemonade or preferred something else.

"*Na*, I am okay with it," he said.

Hearing a new male voice at home, Daddy came out of his room to see who had come. As Daddy came out Kabir and me stood up.

"Daddy I was just about to call you. Meet my friend Kabir, he is in my college."

"Hello young man, how are you doing?"

"I am good uncle, how about you?"

Daddy hesitated a bit while answering. Saying that you are not at all fine to a person you are meeting for the first time was not a good idea.

"I'm good too. Make yourself comfortable and feel like home. Nidhi I hope you've offered him something."

I just nodded.

I don't know what came to Kabir's mind. He went closer to Daddy to have a conversation.

"Uncle, isn't it getting really hot this summer?"

"I haven't stepped out of home in the last few days, but yes I saw the current temperature in the weather forecast. It's pretty hot outside, although I don't feel it as I spend most of the time at home with air conditioners on."

"Yes but for those who do not have air conditioners or air coolers, it's really hard for them in such hot weather."

Daddy was muddled and so was I. What exactly was Kabir trying to do?

"I just visited Vindur with Nidhi. Some of them were okay with the fans but some of them were having a hard time because a few fans weren't in a proper condition. And after mummy, they have no one to look after them."

Was Kabir pouring salt on Daddy's wounds or was he trying to help daddy? I was totally blank.

"Uncle there are many along with you who are missing mom and whose life has become extremely difficult after mom's death. For you, nobody can replace mom, but for them it can be you.

Daddy, can you give them a godfather in compensation for losing their godmother?"

Daddy's eyes were filled with tears.

"Beta there is no one like her, and there can never be someone like her..."

"Daddy I am sure what you are saying is true, and who can know this better than you. But, since you knew her the most, you can play her part the best, isn't it?"

While talking Kabir didn't realise that he was addressing daddy as daddy instead of uncle.

"Daddy you'll do it *na*...? Oh, I'm sorry... Uncle."

He said the word uncle with a long pause.

"Daddy is fine. You can call me daddy. And..."

Daddy took a big pause

"Yes, I will do it."

I could see the spirit in Daddy's eyes. As if he found a reason to live. And I didn't expect daddy to agree instantly, the way he'd behaved after mummy's death. But it was a welcome relief for me. "I'll go there tomorrow and will personally monitor their needs and difficulties. In fact, I'll try and go every day."

It didn't look like they had met for the first time. Their chemistry filled me with pleasure. I was glad, at least something worked for daddy. After this I fell for Kabir even more strongly. I was lost in Kabir and therefore, did not hear them speaking after that. Kamla *kaaki* called me twice for lemonade but I was oblivious to everything. Finally, Kabir touched the cold glass of lemonade on my hand which made me quiver slightly and I was back to my senses.

"Nidhi, your drink," he said.

Daddy asked Bhushan to drop Kabir home or to college, wherever he wanted to go.

That night I was thinking of Kabir and thought of messaging him. It was 1' a.m. Should I? Shouldn't I? Should I? Shouldn't I? I wasted an hour deciding whether or not to message him. I finally texted him on WhatsApp.

"There?"

He immediately replied.

"Ya... all good? Daddy is fine *na*?"

"Yes..yes all good...in fact, today he has smiled after days. All thanks to you."

"I'm glad I could help."

"Kabir…"

"Say *na*…"

"Sure?"

"Of course!"

"I have been thinking of you a little more than I should."

"Should I tell you something too?"

"Yes Of course!"

"I haven't passed a minute without thinking of you ever since I've been in touch with you."

I was blushing from within when I heard this. My happiness knew no bounds.

"Really?"

"*Na*, just kidding…"

😢

"Have you ever felt this way before?"

"Ya ya, I feel this for every other girl."

😢 "go"

"Come *na*…"

"Where?"

"Wherever you asked me to go."

"Kabir please be serious."

"Ok. I love you"

He said 'I Love you' so easily...! Is this the case with everyone? Was it very quick? Or he wanted to say it long back and it's too late? What is happening between us?

I was engulfed by these thoughts.

"This isn't a prank right?"

"If you were able to see yourself through my eyes, you wouldn't have asked this."

"Okay."

"What okay?"

"You love me...okay"

"You won't tell me your feelings for me?"

"No."

"Okay goodnight then."

"What goodnight? You can't even insist or what?"

"I know you'll tell me anyway."

"I love you Kabir. I really do."

"Is it? How much?"

I didn't reply to him for half an hour, he was wondering if I slept or what exactly I was up to? He sent me a message after half an hour. "Slept?"

Still no reply from my side. I replied after a while. I sent him an image of a page which had a few handwritten words for him.

You asked me how much I love you

I wanted to say, to the moon and back

I wanted to say, I love you to eternity

I wanted to say, how much I love you is like counting stars- impossible

I wanted to say I love you with each and every breath I take and till the last one.

But I didn't say any of these, coz I actually don't know how to weigh love.

I don't know why I want to see you immediately after you've just left.

I don't know why I want to talk to you after you've just hung up.

I don't know why it sucks when you don't talk to me or when you are not around.

I don't know why I want to hear as many times as you say you love me.

I don't know why anything good or bad doesn't matter to me anymore.

I don't know why I don't fear death anymore.

I don't know why I wake up in the middle of the night and find you sleeping beside me.

I don't know why I feel like doing everything possible that makes you happy.

I just know that I feel for you and probably the best word to describe the feeling is love…

I love you…how? Since when? Why? How much? I don't know…

"Ohhhh baby…I'm speechless… I love you… you are the best thing that's ever happened to me…

Acha tell me something…

You spent 50 mins searching on google or you wrote this on your own :p?"

😊 "I wrote this for you."

"That day it was my first kiss."

"Is it? I can't exactly recall the count."

"Ohhh..."

"Kidding Nidhi, it was my first kiss too."

It was 3 a.m. I gave him a call.

He didn't even wait for a single ring to go. He immediately picked up.

"Yes baby."

I didn't want to play around the bush, so I directly told him,

"I want to meet you."

"Morning we are meeting in college, right?"

"Now."

"Now?" he said surprised.

"It's really late I know but I want to meet you now, I can't wait to see you. Hang up and come to my place right away. Give me a call once you reach, I'll come to receive you at the gate."

"Is it safe?"

"Kabir I've taken care of everything, you just come over."

Kamla *kaaki* and daddy were fast asleep, and I knew even the watchman took a long nap at this time. I knew this because after mummy's death, I had spent many sleepless nights sitting in my balcony, looking for her amongst stars like a kid.

I was startled as my phone buzzed; it was him. I started trembling with the thought that he was around. I could not wait to see him. I had a look into the mirror, ran my fingers into my hair, took a deep breath and trying to hide my smile, I rushed to the gate. It was a full moon night. He was wearing black shorts and a basic white t-shirt. His legs were far fairer than his face and arms. I started blushing as I saw him.

"Nidhi you look very adorable in night wear, this pink colour compliments your skin." I could not say anything. This usually happened to me when he was around. My heart was so content that I barely felt like saying anything at all. I heard him but did not respond most of the time, and at times I was so lost that I barely heard him. At times it so happened that I'd have so much to compliment him, but because I went speechless, I never expressed my feelings for him. He waited for me to say anything if not thank you. 'At least let's go inside.' I kept on staring at him and he interrupted me, "is this it?"

I had a question mark on my face.

"I mean you just called me for this at this time of the night? We are not going in, right?"

"Ohh! I am so sorry. Let's go in." He parked his bike and we started walking in. I wanted to hold his arm and take him in. I really wanted to but was too shy. We reached the living room and he asked, raising his eyebrows, "What next?"

I pointed to the bedroom.

"Are you sure?"

"Yes."

I had dimmed my bedroom lights. As he entered, I locked the door.

I turned to him after locking the door, he said, "so am I now allowed to ask what I am here for?"

I started blushing. I went closer to him, putting my hands on his chest and whispered, "To love me." He brought me closer, pulling me by my waist. My body quivered. I started taking long, deep breaths. He hugged me tight, I could hear his heartbeat. My hands were now around his neck, he tightened the grip over me and lifted me up. I never wanted to come out of his arms. My joy knew no bounds. I whispered in his ear, "I love you Kabir."

"I love you much more Nidhi."

He slowly brought his lips to my neck. I started palpitating. After leaving a few deep kisses on my neck, he started looking into my eyes, I fluttered my eyes. He raised my chin with his cold hands. His hands were cold as he had come on a bike at this time of night. My lips met his and they locked. I clutched him tightly when he started playing with my tongue. He nibbled my lower lip. While kissing me he said, "I always wondered which part of your lips is tastier, the upper one or the lower one." He did not want any answer, our lips met again. Soon his hands ran inside my t-shirt, he unhooked my bra. I gave him a slight push and just said, "Kabir". He immediately removed his hand from my t-shirt and took a step back. After a few seconds I took his hands and enfolded them on my waist and I started kissing him passionately from his forehead to eyes, then to his cheeks. He stopped me and asked me in a sensuous tone.

"What do you want me to do Nidhi?"

I did not know what to say.

"If you continue to be in my arms for some more time, then I won't be able to control myself, so tell me if I should leave immediately or shall I stay back?" I did not answer. I was feeling shy. Since I didn't answer, he loosened his grip over me and started stepping back. I pulled him back over me and said, "I am all yours baby." He then lifted me in his arms and took me to bed. He was in my arms. We started kissing and cuddling amorously. First, he took off his t-shirt and then started undressing me. I could not resist moaning when he touched my breasts. We were on fire. Within no time we both were completely naked, buried into each other's bodies. I could not believe it was happening to me. I was about to lose my virginity. When he was just about to enter me, I stopped him.

"What about protection Kabir?"

"Nidhi, I did not anticipate us going so far tonight so did not carry any protection!"

"So now what?"

"What now what!!! You can't divest me of you now. I told you I won't be able to hold myself after this!"

He took a deep breath and said, "Okay I won't force you if you are not comfortable doing it without protection."

"And if I want you to force me?" I said, giving him a naughty smile.

No man on earth would stop after hearing what I said. We made love. The pleasure was ultimate but at the same time it was painful too, and it took many attempts, maybe because it was our first time. I was quietly lying in his arms after we were done.

I wasn't asleep, neither was he but we did not speak a word, we were just cherishing the moment. We were relaxed but became a little cautious at the crack of dawn. "I should leave Nidhi," he said. I just gave him an agreeing nod. Although I did not want him to go but his staying longer wouldn't have been safe either. While leaving he hugged me, kissed my forehead and he said, "No need to attend college today, take rest."

"Hmmm!"

I dropped him to the gate. I came back to my bedroom. I was feeling full of joy from within. I wasn't feeling sleepy at all. I hugged my pillow and fell asleep after a while.

I slept till 12 noon that day. *Kaaki* and daddy were worried. They thought I was unwell so I slept for so long. *Kaaki* came to enquire, I told her I was working on a project till late night so I wanted to sleep. After talking to me, they both breathed a sigh of relief. I asked *kaaki* not to disturb me for brunch or lunch. "I will wake up and ask for it whenever I'm hungry." I was awake after 12, but was still in bed for a very long time. In the afternoon I received a call from Mahira. I was wondering why she had called. Was it because she saw us together? What if she confronts me directly? But why am I bound to answer her? Mahira was never in a relationship with Kabir. I don't owe her any explanation. Before I could answer the call, the call disconnected. She called again after 5 mins, I received it immediately.

"Hey Mahira!"

"Hi Nidhi, why didn't you receive my call earlier?"

"You had called? I was in the washroom. Sorry I didn't notice your call."

"Oh okay, no problem, why didn't you come to college today?"

"Had something to do at home so didn't come. You tell me, how did you call?"

"I just called to invite you to my place for a movie and dinner tonight."

"Sounds good, but why all of a sudden?"

"Ya it's a sudden plan. All our friends are coming. So be here by 7."

"Sure, see you then."

"Bye."

I immediately called Kabir.

"Yes Nidhi, we'll go there by 7."

I was happy at the thought of meeting him again.

"See you."

While in the car I asked Kabir, "Yesterday when Mahira saw us together, she seemed annoyed, she might react to it now. Do you think it's okay to visit her place or should we make some excuse?"

"I can proudly accept you as my girlfriend before everyone, provided you want to accept it too. So, I don't mind answering her if she confronts us." His reply brought back the missing confidence inside me. I loved it when he called me, 'mine'. "You went speechless again Nidhi. Most of the time when I speak, I see you blushing or speechless instead of replying to me."

"So, you don't like it that way?"

"*Na*... I love it..."

We reached Mahira's house. Everyone was already there; she gave us a warm welcome unlike I'd expected. I thought maybe I had misjudged her. When we entered, we saw a huge music room at her house with a wide screen which gave a theatre-like feeling.

The room had a red carpet across the floor and three long steps in a curved design with cushions and mats on each step meant for sitting. A few bean bags were randomly kept at the corners. Everyone was seated as per their convenience and comfort. Kabir and I chose to sit at the corner holding cushions in our hands. As the movie started, Mahira turned off the lights. After half an hour, everyone was watching the movie very intently. Kabir slowly slid his hand into my top from behind. He started titillating my back. I was enjoying his hand on my body. I had gripped his t-shirt very tight. We were not at all interested in watching the movie. Mahira suddenly turned back towards us. We got conscious. She stood up immediately. Aditi asked her, "What happened?"

"Movie is incomplete without popcorn and snacks, I'll get them for all."

I said, "I'll come to help you."

"Sure."

We went to the kitchen but there was nothing to do. Her staff had kept everything ready and they were about to serve popcorn, nuggets, samosas and cold drinks to all. Mahira instructed them to start serving.

"All done?" I asked

She hesitated a bit and said, "aaamm!! Not actually, I had brought a few candies and chocolates for all, they are in my room. Will you get them?"

"Sure."

"My room is upstairs, last one to the left, the chocolates are in a brown cover."

She was doing something on her phone while instructing me and looked nervous. I, on the other hand, was confused as to why she sent me to get the chocolates when she was idle too. Nevertheless, I went to get them.

As I entered the room the lights suddenly went off, and the room was totally dark. I was wondering how there could be a power cut at 'The-oh-so-rich-Mahira's residence.' The moment I turned back, someone locked the door. I got scared, I started calling for Mahira. No one responded. I kept on shouting for help. It was because the room was upstairs, no one was able to hear me. My phone was left in the music room. I had no idea what to do. But I was sure if I don't return back in a while, Mahira would come looking for me.

Kabir got a little worried, he enquired for me from Aditi.

"Hey where is Nidhi?"

"Oh oh...why so worried aa?" She said teasing him.

"Not worried, I just asked, where is she Mahira?" He asked Mahira.

"She is coming in a while."

"ok."

Someone pounced on me from behind. I could sense a bad touch. I immediately groped for the door handle and tried to unlock it. I started shouting loudly for help.

Kabir became a little more anxious about me. It had been fifteen minutes. He stood up. Mahira asked him, "What happened Kabir?"

"I just want to go to the washroom."

As he came out of the music room, he heard my voice and he immediately reached out to the room. He tried opening the door but was unable to do so. He screamed for Mahira. She pretended as if she didn't hear it. She increased the volume deliberately so that no one else could hear us scream. But fortunately, before she raised the volume, Aditi heard Kabir shouting out for help. She asked Mahira to lower the volume or turn it off instead. She refused. Aditi told her aggressively, 'I heard Kabir calling you and that too not normally. I sense something weird is happening out there.' She rose up and even the rest of them. They rushed to the room. Kabir asked Mahira to open the door immediately. She just nodded and called out to her maid to get her the room key. The person who was abusing me escaped from the window as he heard the clamour. The moment the door opened I hugged Kabir very tightly, I was overstrung with all that had happened. Everyone else was distraught except Mahira. Kabir asked me about what happened, I told him in a whimpering tone the whole thing. He just looked at Mahira with a suspicious eye, held my hand and said, "Let's leave."

By now the picture was almost clear for everyone, they all were dumbfounded. We left the place at once. Kabir was irate with Mahira's actions. But he then thought pacifying me was more important at that time. He pulled me towards him, hugging me he started apologising.

"Baby I am always there. I won't let anything happen to you till I am there. I am sorry I was a bit late, I am really sorry honey."

"I love you Kabir, never leave me alone."

"Love you much more baby."

It was lucid that Mahira did this out of a feeling of resentment. But Kabir and I thought of forgetting all this and moving ahead. Mahira never apologised or talked about what she did. We thought she must be guilty. We avoided meeting and talking to her after that day. But we never shared a fuming glance with her when we accidentally came across. We just smiled and walked off.

That night after the incident as I reached home, I sent an image of a hand written note to Kabir.

I know neither I am exquisite, nor I am exemplary.

At times I am irksome, at times I am pesky...

A day I'll crinkle, a day I'll be time-worn

Sometimes I'll daunt you, sometimes I'll turn you on...

I will always try to make you roll in the aisles

But I may drive you scatty against my wills...

The days will turn out in nights and nights to days in turn

I won't be able to change myself but I am certain...

My love for you will never ever change ...

Coz for me you are something words can't state...

He gave me a call after reading the note.

"How are you my doll?"

"I'm good, baby."

"I wanna go out with you tomorrow."

I knew he wanted to soothe me. And I really wanted him to.

"We'll go out, but not to a restaurant or something. Somewhere where we can be alone."

"Sure darling, wherever you say."

We went to Osho garden at Koregaon Park.

I just can't let you go

We were sitting on a bench, I was deep in my thoughts, not making any contact with Kabir and just facing the sky, then I spoke, "Kabir I have visited the best places in the world. I've had a variety of food from almost every corner of the world. At this age I've experienced and visited so many beautiful things and places which many people can only dream of, but you know, what I feel with you it's... it's just ultimate, divine! I literally forget the world when I'm in your arms. But you know what, in the initial days of our relationship I used to feel very happy but the more I'm coming closer to you, I am scared, scared of losing you. If destiny seizes you from me, where will I go, what will I do? I am ill at ease due to this thought." I started panicking. My eyes filled with tears almost ready to spill.

"Don't panic sweetie, I am going nowhere. I am right here with you today, tomorrow and always. No one can seize me from you."

"You don't know Kabir destiny sometimes plays so well, that we have no option but to give up and surrender against our will. I know you will never wish to, neither will I but what if it still happens?"

"Nidhi if it happens just remember, wherever I might be, in whatever state, I will always love you. You will always be my last wish. Your smiling face will always be my strength and my ultimate happiness."

He held my cheeks, looking deep into my eyes, brought me a little closer and very softly and tenderly sucked the tears flowing down my eyes. I just lost myself in him. I rested my hands on his broad chest.

"I never want to see them in your eyes again," he said.

We just couldn't stop ourselves from kissing each other. But Kabir was cautious. He didn't allow the kiss to last for more than 10 seconds.

Pulling his collar and giving that naughty smile I said, "I don't like this on you," signalling towards his shirt.

"Oh ohh...girls in the garden will lose control if I take off my shirt."

"The property inside the shirt is mine. Only mine."

"This is not our bedroom Nidhi."

"But the car is all ours and fortunately it's a no moon day."

"You know, I once heard our elders talking about no intercourse on a no moon day."

"Shhhh!!! Quietly get into the car or else get ready to be ripped and raped."

"Go ahead I am ready. I am not getting into the car."

"Go...I'm not talking to you."

I stood up and started moving to the car. He pulled me from my waist and kissed my neck from behind, then opened the door for me.

The space inside the car wasn't comparable to that of a bed, but the idea of making love in the car was rather thrilling.

"Ohh I love you so much Kabir..."

"Love you much more Nidhi..."

"Kabir are you serious, we are gonna eat junk from a roadside vendor?" He took me to a roadside hawker as I was hungry. But I couldn't imagine eating street food as I wasn't sure if it was hygienic. He said the grilled sandwich there was very tasty and he loved eating it. He knew I was reluctant to try street food, but he still wanted me to try it. And I was so madly in love with him that it was very difficult to say a no to him for anything. Although there was a considerable difference between our status but we never had any conflict of interest or a huge difference of opinion about anything. But it's not that we never fought. In fact, we fought very frequently, that too, mainly when I skipped meals or didn't take proper rest. Most of the time it was because of me. He seldom gave me a chance to complain.

"Give us two cheese grilled sandwiches," Kabir said, as the man was serving the other customer.

"Two! Kabir do you think by any chance I can finish this whole sandwich. Just look at the size of the sandwich he is making."

"Don't worry darling, I know you can't finish it completely but I can have half of yours as well. I am hungry too. Mom wasn't well today, so I asked her not to cook. I assured her that I'd manage my own breakfast and lunch"

"Ohh", I was worried because of what he said.

I started fighting with him because of his carelessness.

"You could have told me that you were hungry. We could have bunked a class today. You never tell me anything about yourself and that's what bothers me the most. Kabir I love the attention and care you give me. I love the way you pamper me. But give me a chance to do the same for you. If not always at least sometimes. You don't know how much you matter to me. I might not make out from your face like you do, and that's where you have to cooperate."

"I know you love me sweetie. But I can handle it, trust me. I don't like to bother you for everything. And I know when I need you, you'll cross the seven seas for me. You are not weak at all. You are my girl. The would-be Mrs. Kabir Gandhi…"

I was blushing when he said this. He always knew how to cheer me up. He was truly a charmer.

"What would I do without you Kabir?"

"Ummm!!! Lemme think. You can miss me without me," he smiled.

"No, I never want to do that. I always want you with me."

Our sandwiches were ready. Just after I had my first bite I spoke while my mouth was still full. "It's yummm Kabir."

"You liked it?"

"Yes, a lot."

"I am glad."

Kabir smiled and humorously said to the man who prepared the sandwich, "*Bhaiyaji* if our madam liked your sandwich, it means your sandwich got a national certification. She is no less than a food inspector."

I gave him a pat on his shoulder as he was teasing me. The man said he was glad that I liked it.

The way that man spoke to Kabir, brought in a question. "You visit him frequently?"

"*Na na*, not that frequently."

"It seemed so, the man seems really familiar with you."

Although I was speaking in a hushed tone, the man somehow managed to hear what we were saying and answered me before Kabir could.

"Madam, *bhaiyaji* is one of those people who always leave their mark behind. I am sure he certainly strikes a rapport with everyone he meets."

I couldn't agree more, and at the same time felt very proud.

I was watching him with naughty eyes.

"Now don't ogle at me like this," he said teasing me.

I burst out laughing when he said this, "What? I am ogling at you…? Looks like you are enjoying it too."

By the way you never told me about your family, your mom?"

"There are three of us at home, me and my parents."

"So, you are the only child?"

"No, I have a sister, Tamanna. She is married and settled with her husband and her daughter Pihu, in London."

"Oh! London…!" I said in amazement, "Does she visit frequently?"

"It's been four years since she's gone, she hasn't come even once."

"Ohh…you must be missing her."

"Yeah, a lot."

"What does your father do?"

"He has a cycle store."

"You don't go help him at the store."

"Barely, I go only when he asks for it."

"So your mom stays back at home alone all day?"

"Ya, no other option."

"So if she isn't well, who cooks for you all?"

"Swiggy."

"Ohh... good. I want to see where you live."

'Now?'

"Yes."

"But sweetheart mom is not well today, she won't be able to welcome you properly today, and even the house must be a mess. Why not some other day?"

"No, no. You got me wrong. We won't go into your house. I just want to see it from the outside. At least I should know where you live *na*, to sue you in case you cheat on me."

"Oh oh...You and your ideas...Okay come let's go."

We usually commuted on his bike. I never wanted to miss a chance to be close to him. That's why we barely used my car to travel.

Kabir lived in a 2bhk row house. There were eight bungalows in a row. Although they were small in size, they were well maintained and beautiful.

We stood near a bungalow which was two bungalows before his house because he didn't want his mom to see us. Kabir said that with the thunder that his bike made, mummy understood that he was back home. There was a very pretty girl standing on the balcony of the bunglow where we stood. She called Kabir loudly, waved at him and gave him a flying kiss.

My instant reaction was, "Awww! This kiddo looks like a doll!"

"Isn't she, she is my darling."

"Rihanna, come down," Kabir said.

She came down in no time. Her mom followed her to see where she was heading at such a fast pace. We were on the bike itself. As she came close to us, Kabir leaned forward to kiss her on her forehead, she kissed him back on his cheek. She was so adorable and her voice was the sweetest voice I'd ever heard. Her mom came behind and said in a loud and monotone , "I've told you a hundred times Rihu to call him bhaiya not Kabir."

She nodded her face in resentment and said, "Never! I am going to marry him when I grow young." We all laughed together in amusement.

Kabir held her, and whispered something in her ears.

"The girl sitting behind is trying to steal your boyfriend."

She instantly frowned at me. She seemed really annoyed.

Although she seemed annoyed from within, Rihanna did not react. Probably because I was a complete stranger to her. But her hostility towards me was inevitably visible and she looked cute at the same time. "Kabir is mine. You go away. You are bad."

"No sweetheart I am just a friend, he is teasing you, he is all yours. I don't like him anyway."

"Better," she said.

Kabir asked her leave as he had to drop me.

On our way home, he asked me, "Was it necessary to add, I don't like him anyways. So, this is the fact..?"

"What? Of course it is, I don't like you, you have trapped me in your love."

He abruptly applied brakes to his bike which pushed me closer to him. He turned back to look into my eyes, as if he wanted to verify what I said.

I was completely in a mischievous mood. He knew it well, and still pretended to be annoyed.

As he turned towards me, I kissed his cheek a little harder than usual. I patted his back with my hand indicating that he should move ahead. "Let's go, you know I love you."

Everything had started falling into place. The wounds in our hearts of losing mom had not vanished completely but the pain accompanied with it seemed to mitigate slowly. And the sole reason was Kabir. He was a saviour. His presence in my life had changed things drastically. Not only me, even Daddy felt the same. My meetings with Kabir became more frequent. The nights which I spent crying, now passed on phone calls. I spoke to him for hours, sometimes till dawn broke. His presence in my life was magic. I always thanked God, for he had been so generous to send Kabir into my life.

Winters were approaching. One fine day we just thought of going for a night walk. We were ambling close to my home. Actually, he had come to drop me home after we had dinner together. I told him that I wanted some more quality time with him. Then he suggested we go for a walk. It was Diwali eve. The whole city was lit. Everyone had decorated their homes with beautiful lights, diyas and lanterns. Many of them had started bursting crackers already. Although it was pleasant being around family on such an auspicious day, I wanted to be alone with him. That evening reminded me of my last Diwali with mom. That's why we went a bit far from the hustle and bustle of the ongoing celebrations. It was pretty cold that night. I was shivering due to the chill breeze. The situation was like a scene from a Bollywood movie. Kabir was just about to remove his jacket and drape it over me but I stopped him. He was a little confused.

"You are shivering out of cold baby."

"Yes I am."

"Are you being formal with me?"

"How can I be formal with you?"

"Then why don't you allow me to wrap my jacket around you?"

I dragged him towards me by pulling both ends of his jacket, then I slipped my hands slowly around his waist inside his jacket and embraced him.

"I want this warmth baby."

It's strange isn't it? when one person means the world to you and the whole world becomes invisible "You are my world Kabir, you are everything I have. I surrender myself to you in this life and all the lives coming my way. I can't play with words as easily as you do, but you can read my eyes, they won't ever lie to you. You will always find yourself in them. They are full of you."

When we were quiet for a while, Kabir said he wanted to talk about something.

"Say *na*..."

"Yesterday one of the aunts from our neighbourhood invited mom to her place as her would be, daughter-in-law was supposed to come for Laxmi pooja. After the lady left mom was discussing Laxmi pooja with me and Daddy."

"Daughters in law are believed to be the *Laxmis* of our homes. If the daughter in law herself does Laxmi pooja at home on Diwali, it's believed to bring good luck to the family. I wish we had her with us for the pooja this year." My parents were looking at me for an answer.

I said, "What? Why are you looking at me like this? It's not my job to find a daughter-in-law for you, you can go and hunt for one."

Mom said, "We don't have to hunt for one."

"Why?"

"I like that Padma's daughter for you. I've already spoken to her about you."

I was dumbfounded. The pitch of my voice automatically increased as I was annoyed listening to all this. "How could you talk to aunty without my consent? I love Nidhi," I said.

Both mum Daddy burst out laughing, and I was embarrassed. I avoided eye contact with them. Mom started running her hand in my hair with affection. She said, "As if we didn't know anything, haan! Your late-night talks, the way you smile for no reason, that different spark in your eyes. I am your mother; I can read your eyes since your birth. Bring her home for *pooja* tomorrow if it's convenient for her."

"Kabir I am already nervous."

"Don't be baby. My parents are very jolly and warm. You won't feel uneasy at all. You'll come *na*?"

"Certainly."

"Wow *Kaaki*, the *rangoli* looks amazing! Looks like you've drawn this."

"Yes, of course," she said with a big smile, facing Kabir.

There was a big *rangoli* at the entrance, she had drawn a beautiful peacock design. And the lamps and candles, she'd placed around it had enhanced its beauty even more.

Kaaki always wore a smile on her face as if she was constantly being clicked in pictures. But it gave a very warm feeling to every guest who walked into our house. After all she was the one who appeased us and the guests too. Kabir bowed down to touch her feet and give her Diwali wishes. He gave her a box of sweets.

She said, "I'll give this to baby. Wait, I'll call her, she must be ready."

"No *Kaaki* I've got others for Nidhi as well; these are for you and your family."

She felt honoured. Kabir always knew how to do it. He always managed to create a very affectionate bond with everyone who came across him. He then asked *Kaaki* about her family and how she was planning to celebrate Diwali with her family. She held his face between her palms and said, "Nidhi is lucky to have you in her life. You are a very nice guy."

He just smiled in response. I was already there watching them both, but they did not notice me.

I interrupted their conversation. In a loud naughty tone, I said, "Isn't he lucky to have me *Kaaki*?"

"Of course, he is" she said, "He is gonna own a real gem, one in a zillion." I came forward to hold her in my arms with love.

Kabir looked very handsome in traditional attire too. Sometimes I felt like putting a tag which said that he was mine, so that I could save him from every girl eyeing on him. He was wearing a pista green kurta and off-white pyjamas with Kolhapuri chappals. And that ring on his left ear always complemented his looks.

"Nidhi you look ravishing in this lehenga."

"I know... tell me something I don't know"

He grinned.

"Shall we go?"

"Yes, just a moment," I called out to Bhushan to help me put some stuff in my car.

"*Kaaka* put all these sweets and gifts in my car."

Not in your car Nidhi," Kabir said.

"We can't go on your bike Kabir, I am wearing a lehenga."

I know darling, he slightly pulled my hand to take me out to show me something.

It was a new car; it was his new car.

"Ohh...you got a new car", I shouted with elated emotions! "You didn't mention at any point that you are buying a new one."

"This is a surprise gift from my father. He said, 'if you told me earlier that you are travelling with your girlfriend all over the city on your bike, I would have got you one long ago.'"

"He is a cool father. I am really excited about meeting them both."

I shouted with glee, "*Kaka* put the stuff in Kabir's car."

The boot of the car and the backseat as well were crammed with the stuff I had got for them.

"What is all this Nidhi?", he asked as he was uncertain about what was happening.

"This is for you all and Rihu."

"You mean all these sweets, crackers and gifts are for us?"

I nodded.

"Nidhi one or two gifts and a few sweets are ok, but these many sweets…? What do you want? Shall we not cook at home for the coming month and fill our tummies with sweets alone? I mean we are just three of us at home, that too one of them is diabetic."

"I was really confused as to which one was the best, that's why I got them all."

"Okay come let's go, we'll share this with our neighbours and a few kids who stay in a nearby slum. This way we can share our joy and the sweets won't be wasted either."

"My baby," I said giving him a pout, "Let's go."

"Happy 'Sweetali'," he said in a kiddish tone as it was more of sharing sweets, his mom had even sent some homemade ones for me.

We reached his home. His mom had put a ready to use rangoli sticker. As she did not have a helping hand at home, the ready sticker was convenient for her. That looked beautiful in its own sweet way. Honestly speaking, I was really nervous when I was about to meet them. The moment his mom saw me, she commented, "You are just a piece of moon." She hugged me after saying this. I suddenly started missing my mom due to which my eyes were moist. Everyone became quiet.

"Hey what happened?" Kabir asked in a worried tone.

"Nothing, I am fine."

"Come on tell me."

"Just missing mom."

Kabir had told his parents that I had recently lost my mom, hence they already knew about it. His mom took me in her arms, "Although we can't bring her back but I can certainly replace her with me."

Her words made me feel much better. His parents were gems at heart. I was feeling blessed to have them all. We finished the pooja, followed by the bursting crackers. Rihanna and some other kids in the neighbourhood joined us. We gave chocolates to all of them. Rihaana's share was the biggest, her eyes shone with pleasure as if chocolates were her first love.

We had so much fun with crackers. Bursting crackers is the most awaited wind of excitement that Diwali brings. The sparkling fire shooting cracker, which flashed on the ground in a whirling motion amazed the little kids. As soon as the blazing whirlpool began, the kids jumped on the sparks. They held pencil crackers, and watching them under the skies filled with flying lamps were a treat to the eyes. Kids were scared to light the fireworks because of which every time they wanted me or Kabir to do it. I was so bothered with my long and wavy skirt, and its heavy weight that I was not in a position to light them. Instead, I enjoyed watching Kabir do it. *How I love him!,* my heart said, every time I saw him smiling. Although we were happy, and the moment was perfect, it had to come to an end. I had to reach home early as even Daddy was waiting for me for pooja.

I couldn't have asked for anything better on that day. As we reached home, *bhai* was waiting to surprise me. My joy knew no bounds. I went running towards him and hugged him tight.

"We've missed you so badly *bhai*."

"I don't think so, your calls to me have gradually reduced, and I know what's the reason behind it."

Bhai's statement made me nervous for a while.

"Don't worry. Daddy has told me about Kabir, my princess has grown up now and has learnt how to efficiently hide things from her elder brother."

"No *bhai*! I thought I would speak to you about this when we meet. It wasn't deliberate."

"I know it *Gudda*. And now that I've come, I would like to meet him."

He was standing at the door, not wanting to disturb our conversation.

"You won't have to wait any longer for that, he is here," I said pointing towards the door where he was standing.

Bhai was really happy to see him.

Kabir and I had completed the long pending tasks of meeting each other's family which was very easy and pleasant contrary to what we had expected.

Wednesday, December 20, 10:30 p.m

It had been many days since we'd last met. He was busy training Rihanna for an upcoming dance competition at her school. And she wanted only Kabir to train her. In fact, Kabir was the best choice to make because he had excellent dancing skills.

It was a freezing winter night and I loved winters, the skies filled with stars, the sense of relief I felt when the cool breeze touched my body, sleeping under cosy blankets, hot coffees, I just loved the season. I was in my balcony savouring the moment.

Kabir's call was an icing on the cake.

"Hi baby."

"Hey honey..."

"What are you doing?"

"On my balcony, relishing this beautiful evening."

"Enjoying without me, *haan*?"

I chuckled, "Come and hug me to make the evening more beautiful with your presence."

"*Na*, I won't come to hug you."

I was muddled, he continued, "Today you are going to hug me tight...we'll go on a ride on my bike."

"Sounds great."

"Take your bluetooth speaker along, I want to dedicate a song to you"

"Okay, I am waiting *shon*, bye."

"Bye darling."

He got ready immediately, wearing his jacket, helmet and biker gloves. He wanted to breathe free, he wanted to feel my hug very closely. He left saying this. We were on call, while he was on his way. Rihanna saw him going somewhere and she called out loud from her balcony, "Kabir." He stopped promptly.

"Hey doll."

"Where to Kabir?"

"Nowhere specific."

"Let's go have an ice cream."

Her mom came from behind saying, "No one is going out at this time. You are already exhausted with dance practice. You need rest, you have to perform tomorrow. And anyway, you have already brushed your teeth, so no ice cream. Go some other day."

"That's what I am trying to say mumma, I am already exhausted and I really need a refreshment," Rihanna said in a convincing tone.

Rihanna was too smart for her age.

Kabir said, "Let her go aunty I'll bring her back within half an hour."

Her mom agreed when Kabir insisted.

Her mom asked Kabir to wait for a minute, perhaps she wanted Rihanna to wear her jacket.

Meanwhile he said, "Baby listen *na*, I am sorry I'll be a little late."

"That's ok but what happened? All good?"

"Ya ya, all good, Rihanna wants to have an ice cream so I am taking her for that, you know I can never say no to her."

"So, three of us can't go together?"

"We can, but the problem is your house is too far and the ice cream van is just ten minutes away. If I come to pick you, Rihanna will be very late for bed and it's her dance performance at school tomorrow. She has been practising for so many days. She needs proper sleep, hope you understand."

"I completely do, wish her luck on my behalf. See ya."

"Can't wait to see you, anyways, bye."

Rihanna came running.

"Easy, easy, doll."

"We'll go to that ice cream van Kabir."

"I already knew you would want to go there."

Kabir lifted her and made her sit in the front space of the bike facing towards the road.

"I'll have a four-layer ice cream. Vanilla, strawberry, mango and chocolate."

I just can't let you go

"Look at your size, will you be able to have it all alone? Better we'll share the ice cream."

"No, no, no! Although I love you, no sharing ice creams. Rules are rules."

"Okay my little smart granny."

"What will you have Kabir?"

"Plain vanilla scoop sweetie."

"So boring," she said, wrinkling her nose.

They reached the ice cream van.

The uncle at the ice cream van gave them a wide smile as Rihanna was his regular and most adorable customer.

As Kabir spoke to place the order, Rihanna interrupted him shouting with excitement, "Let me place the order." She placed the order for her four-layer ice cream and one boring vanilla ice cream.

Rihanna was drumming on the gas tank of the bike with her hands while she waited for the man to get their ice creams. Rihanna was so eager for her ice cream that she wasn't taking her eyes off the man who was preparing her four layered ice cream cone. Her eyes were sparkling. While her eyes were on the ice cream cone, Kabir kept staring at her. He was glad to see her happy. Rihanna just looked like a barbie doll when she smiled and no wonder, he loved seeing her smile. The moment it was ready, she rubbed her hands to receive it and said in a zeal, "Whoopie!!! Kabir it's ready!"

But what actually happened after that was outrageous.

A car came out of nowhere and hit Kabir's bike from behind with great force. The bike fell down to its left, so did Rihanna and Kabir. Rihanna was hit on the left side of her head and her left elbow was injured too, she was bleeding heavily. But she did not burst out crying like any other child woud, probably because she had lost consciousness due to the stunning blow on her head. Kabir was hit on the head too but not on the elbow as he rested his fist on the ground making an attempt to prevent himself and the bike from falling down but he failed. He was severely injured but still managed to lift himself, the bike and Rihanna too. But as he was trying to lift Rihanna, he was unable to, soon he realised her frock was stuck somewhere in the bike which was making it difficult to lift Rihanna, so he stood first to untangle her frock from the bike.

The phone buzzed. My smile was instinctive because I knew it's going to be him. My cellphone was in my back pocket and I was wearing a headset. I was totally lost in his thoughts and was listening to songs and humming them. I answered the call blindly assuming it's him.

"I am ready baby," I said.

I heard a very tense voice from the other end. A familiar female voice.

"Nidhi, has Kabir come to you?"

For a second, I was dumbfounded. I immediately took out my cell from the pocket to see who it was. It was Dhara didi, Rihu's mom. By the time I could check who it was, she asked me again, "Nidhi have Kabir and Rihanna come to you?"

"He is about to come didi, in fact he'll be here anytime. You sound worried, all good?"

"They both left almost one and a half hours ago. Kabir had told me he'll bring her back within half an hour."

"Don't worry di, I'll call him immediately"

"It's switched off', she bellowed at me, "Why would I call you otherwise?"

I could understand how worried she was. She immediately apologised for being rude.

"Nidhi my heart is sinking, please do something."

"Don't panic didi, I'll go and look for them at the ice cream parlour near your place."

"Even I'll come with you."

"No need didi, it's very late, you please be at home. I am sure they must not have had more than one ice cream, that's why they haven't come yet."

"Hope what you are saying is true, but even then, I want to come with you. Please."

"What about Rihu's Daddy?"

"He hasn't come home yet, he had already informed me about being late today due to some work."

"Okay. I'll leave immediately and pick you up."

Although Dhara di told me that Kabir's phone was switched off, the first thing I did was try his number. To my dismay it was switched off. I left promptly. All the way I was just trying Kabir's number in the hope that maybe the call will get connected. But after so many failed attempts, even I was getting apprehensive. Di was desperately waiting for me outside her gate. She looked so paranoid that I wondered if the situation was actually that serious or this is her general nature. I knew this part of her nature because she had once told me an incident where she gathered all the people in their colony to find Rihanna. She herself too was aggressively searching for her barefoot, with the gas left on in the kitchen. They found Rihanna on the terrace of their place. She loved Rihanna way too much, although every mom does but sometimes when she didn't find her around, she would immediately start panicking. Nevertheless, whatever it was, the need of the hour was to find them first. We both left to search for them. Didi guided me to all the ice cream parlours nearby. All the shops had closed by that time, but even then, we enquired from people around if they had seen Kabir and Rihu. With the increasing number of refusals from people, our hearts began pounding with tension.

"This was the last ice cream parlour I know around," Didi said after we were done asking people in that area.

'The number you have called is either switched off or is out of coverage area', the pre-recorded message said each time I tried his phone.

Didi finally made a call to Rihu's dad. She was stammering when she spoke. She told him everything.

Prabal (Rihanna's father) asked us to leave for home. He said he'll find them, and that it wasn't safe for us to be out alone at this time of the night. As Didi completed her words and hung up, her phone again rang, it was Prabal, "Dhara what did you say? You checked all the ice cream parlours, right?"

"Yes."

"But Rihanna always went to that ice cream van."

"Ice cream van?"

"Yes, yes!" I said interrupting their conversation as I heard the word ice cream van. "Even Kabir had mentioned some van."

"Nidhi is saying Kabir had told her they'll go to some nearby van."

"Okay listen to me, I'll try and reach that place asap, you go home."

"No, let us know where it is, we'll go there too. Please. Please, I insist."

"Okay, okay... relax. That van usually parks at the corner of the crossroad which comes after the hanuman mandir."

"Got it, got it," she said as she quickly recalled the place and hung up the call.

She asked me to start driving immediately, "The place is not even a kilometre away. Let's go."

We rushed to that place, but to our misfortune there was no van over there.

"It was exactly this place Prabal had mentioned," didi said.

The crossroad was not a quiet place. It was a commercial market and I guessed the van generally stood there in the late evening hours after shops were shut. Since those streets always stayed busy, the van easily attracted more customers.

There was a group of boys sitting outside a closed shop. It looked like they were residents of a nearby colony and had gathered to gossip and chit chat after their day's work. I went to them to enquire if they knew about the ice cream van.

"Yes, it stands at this corner," one of the boys said pointing to a corner.

"So hasn't it come today?", I asked.

"It had come but it leaves by this time," one of them said.

Another guy said, "Maybe because of the accident, it has left even earlier."

Didi's eyes widened, she froze when she heard the word accident. She stumbled with shock, but fortunately Prabal just reached there and he held her to save her from falling. He had just arrived, hence he didn't know what the conversation was and why Dhara didi was reacting the way she was.

"Easy Dhara, easy," he said and made her sit on a concrete bench outside a shop. One of the boys ran to get some water for her and he brought it in no time. We gave her some water but she couldn't have it. Her eyes were wide open and she was taking long breaths, she was quivering. I asked the boys what they knew about the accident. I was trying to mollify myself from inside hoping and praying it surely wouldn't be Kabir and Rihanna but I guess I was wrong. The guy said a boy and a seven to eight-year-old girl on a Thunderbird met with an accident when they were waiting for their ice cream, they were brutally hit by a car from behind. Prabhal was still holding himself and he asked for more details.

The guy then properly explained to him with gestures. "The car was taking a right turn on this crossroad and the van was just at the corner itself. It took a very sharp turn. If that bike wouldn't have been there, the car probably would have passed easily. But unfortunately, it dashed the bike with great force."

The other boy interrupted him in an excited tone, "Not only once brother, twice."

The one who was narrating asked, "Twice? How come?"

"When it initially hit the bike, he probably got scared of the crowd rushing towards him. So, he tried to reverse the car and move forward but he couldn't because the bike was on the way. Just about when he was hurrying, he hit the girl's head, not the bike. The boy on the bike was trying to lift the poor girl, failing to which resulted in this horrible incident."

The facts the guys presented hinted that it was Kabir and Rihanna, but my mind was not able to accept and process the truth.

Didi fainted.

Prabhal was still. Silent. Not even a single movement or gesture. Everything seemed like a horrible dream at that moment.

Where are you my love? Where are you Kabir?

"Where are they now?"

"Don't know *taai*." The boys answered unanimously. A man listening to our conversation from behind said, "The owner of Aradhana dresses probably took them to the hospital, you can ask him." The shop was just behind the spot where the van stood.

A boy was quick enough to read the number from the shop board and call him. The man on the other end told him the hospital where he had dropped them.

The boy gave us the details as soon as he hung up. By now it was very clear to the boys that the people who met with the accident were our family. The boy was courteous and was ready to offer us whatever help we needed.

Prabhal folded his hands before me with a trembling body, his eyes filled with tears, "Nidhi, please take Dhara home, I request you. I know you are waiting to see Kabir. But you can see Dhara's condition. Neither we can take her there, nor we can leave her alone. Please! I promise as soon as I come to know anything about them, I'll inform you."

I had no other option but to agree. Prabhal asked the boys to help me with didi, in case she doesn't come back to consciousness. Despite multiple trials, didi was still unconscious. We called for a doctor and gave him their home address so he could give some instant relief to didi. The boys helped me take her home. The doctor arrived after fifteen minutes. He said it was all because of a terrible shock. My main concern was when would she be conscious again to which he replied, "soon she will be conscious on her own." He didn't prescribe any medicine. I was continuously staring at my phone, waiting for Prabhal's call. The phone blinked.

One new message from an unknown number.

I did not have Prabhal's number saved on my phone.

"Our daughter has left us forever.. Kabir has a small injury on his head and is under observation, as soon as I am done with the hospital formalities, I will return home."

He did not have the courage to say this all, which is why he probably chose to message me instead.

Rihanna was no more!

I felt the ground slipping under my feet, I was numb. Before I could digest it all, Didi opened her eyes.

She held my hands tightly, "Where is Rihanna?"

Her intense expressions and the seriousness in her voice scared me, "Tell me!" she shouted.

I could not utter a word. She kept on shouting and asking for Rihu.

Somehow, I mustered the courage to tell her the truth. She obviously could not bear the agony. She started speaking absurd words, "Where must Rihu be Nidhi?" She was sobbing when she said, "Nidhi, please help me find her."

She dragged my hand and started pulling me from one place to another. She dragged me to her study table. "Look Nidhi I can see her here on her little pink chair pretending to write, and scribbling on her table with one hand and playing with the beads of the abacus with the other. Can you see her, tell me...no...can't you? Okay come I'll show you where she is." She took me to the kitchen, "See she is sitting on the kitchen platform and having plain rice in her barbie plate and see she is spilling the curry in the sink. Now she will soon shout saying, 'I finished rice and curry both. See mumma.'" She was laughing a little, then she whimpered and said, "See she is fooling me as if I won't come to know that she spilled the curry. You saw her...no? Not even here...ohh...Nidhi...come. Come here, I will show you."

I had tears in my eyes. I tried to stop her twice, "Didi listen ...", she ignored me and continued her talks and dragged me to Rihanna's washroom, "Oh god this girl she never listens to me. I have told her several times, Rihanna before opening the tap put the bathtub drain plug, but she never listens to me. She turns the taps open and the water continuously flows. I'll close the drainage with a plug. You saw how naughty she is. She will never listen to me and when I yell at her she comes and hugs me and kisses me all over to persuade me."

"Didi please calm down," I shook her vigorously to bring her back to reality.

She started whining and started calling her, "Rihanna ... Rihanna, come back, my child... come back and spill the curry...I won't yell...come and leave the taps open... I won't shout..."

I couldn't stop my tears as I saw her mourn. She was uncontrollable while I tried to console her and hugged her to calm her.

She was sobbing continuously. I found myself helpless. After almost an hour of sniveling, something unforeseen happened. She fainted again and fell down. I was perturbed not only because of what happened but also because there was no one else at home. Rihanna's Daddy had not returned back yet from hospital. He was busy with unending formalities over there. I tried to revive her by sprinkling a few water drops on her face but I failed. I didn't find it convenient to call Rihanna's Daddy as he was already worn out handling hospital formalities especially at that point of time when he himself needed some solace after his daughter's awful demise. Didi regained consciousness after three hours. Those three hours were very challenging. I was yet to break this heart-breaking news before Kabir's parents. I wanted to see Kabir and embrace him, but at the same time I was very sad for Rihu's loss and her parents. As Didi opened her eyes she started speaking. She was facing the ceiling. Her body was still.

"She challenged me, moulded me in many ways. Made me feel elated, invincible. Sometimes it felt like the most frustrating experience ever but every time I lost my temper and yelled at her, just after that I realised how much I loved her and how guilty I felt after shouting at my baby. I fell in love with her before she was born. I felt her presence already. When I was buying her nappies, her t-shirts, I felt as elated as I could ever be. I bought every beautiful colour available. I was already feeling the special fragrance, the beauty of colours, the sound of toys mixed with the laughter of a baby all around. I couldn't hide my feelings while buying all the stuff for my little one. My smile showed my gaiety. The journey started right from the day I came to know that I was expecting. When my delivery time was near, I felt death was better than bearing such labour pains. But today what I am feeling is not even close to death or those pains. The moment she was born, I felt like the whole world was in my hands. The only thing in the whole universe which belonged only to me. I know it was not only mine, it was ours, mine and equally Prabal's. But I gave her birth, she was a part of me which made me overprotective towards her. Each and every bite of fruit, food, each and every drop of milk, juice I fed her was followed with dreams and hopes of making her a strong, healthy and a successful lady. Today I've lost my world."

I had nothing to say to console her. I had never felt so helpless before. The gloomy night somehow passed and dawn broke.

Someone hit the doorbell. I thought the woeful time had come as didi would have to confront Prabal and Rihu's body. I didn't have the courage to open the door. My hands, more precisely, my whole body was quivering. I didn't want to face this at all. *I won't be able to do it alone. I need you Kabir. I desperately need you. I don't even know how you are and what you are going through. Come back and hold me baby. Please come to me. Your Nidhi is not able to do it all alone.*

They banged the door hard as I didn't open it for a minute or two. I went to open the door, it was a lady who looked just like Dhara di, probably her sister. She entered and ignored my presence and reached out for her sister to hold and console her. The others who followed seemed to be their close relatives whom Prabal had called for Rihanna's last rites and cremation ceremony. The whole living room was filled with loud cries.

Rihanna's school bus had arrived to pick her up. They were continuously blowing the horn for Rihanna to come out and board the bus. One of the ladies shouted, will someone please ask them to stop blowing the horn and leave? Our child is no longer alive to attend their school. I went running to the bus. "Please go away."

The bus attendant said, "But how can she miss school today, they have a dance competition today."

I folded my hands before her and said, "Please go away, she is no more."

The attendant was bomb shelled. But there was no point in waiting, with so many kids on board. They had no option but to leave. As I was outside Rihanna's home, the closed door of Kabir's home was clearly visible. I had no choice but to go there and talk to his parents. Initially Kabir's mom used to be awake till he came back. Although he used to be late very often, she used to stay awake for him. But it was in the last few days that she had stopped waiting for him, that too after Kabir's constant insistence. Staying awake for so long was affecting her health due to which Kabir had requested her to sleep on time instead of waiting for him to return. Every time he was late, she knew he'd be with me. But today he was alone, in pain...

I knocked at the door. His mom opened the door. She looked half asleep.

"Ohh! What a surprise my dear," she said yawning; covering her mouth with her hand.

I fell onto my knees before her. She came into consciousness instantly seeing me like this.

"What has happened Nidhi?" she asked, her voice filled with fear. She immediately anticipated something bad had happened. Now that the door was open, she could hear loud

I just can't let you go

cries from Rihu's home. Her blurred fears were now becoming a reality. She could not wait for me to tell her what had happened. Lifting me up in her arms, mom said in a trembling tone, "Speak up Nidhi."

"Mumma...," I was sobbing. I hugged her, she hugged me back. She wanted to soothe me but at the same time she couldn't hold her curiosity filled fears anymore. She wanted to know what had happened.

"My dear please tell me."

"Mumma Kabir and Rihanna met with an accident last night. Kabir is injured but Rihanna..."

"But Rihanna what?"

"Rihanna is no more."

"Where is Kabir?"

"He is in hospital."

"I need to see him immediately. I need to reach him immediately. My son needs me"

Although mom was taken aback hearing about Rihanna's demise, Kabir's news nullified the grief of Rihanna's death. She called out loud for Daddy, "Listen, are you listening to me? Come out right now. We need to go to the hospital." Her scream alarmed me too. I had to rush to the hospital and now that didi had many people who could look after her, I could go see my Kabir. I just hoped that we did not come across Prabal while he brought Rihanna home. I did not have enough energy left to face him. And thankfully, he left the hospital at the same time that we left home. So, we didn't come across him at either of the places.

"Kabir Gandhi?" I enquired at the reception desk. 'Kabir Gandhi...' the lady said raising her eyebrows in confusion and thinking if she had heard this name in the recent past as a patient admitted to her hospital. "Wait, I'll check the records." I interrupted her, "The accident patient who was reported last night..." "Oh that, he is in ICU. You can't meet him now, but you can get more details there. Before that you need to fulfil all the formalities." To which I said, "later" and we straight away rushed to the ICU. There was a nurse inside to look after ICU patients. It had around ten beds inside. She didn't allow us to get in. She said you can't meet the patients here. We could not even see where Kabir was as it was a big room with many beds surrounded with machines on either side.

There was a waiting area outside ICU, so I asked his parents to sit there. The hospital was quiet even during this time of the day. Kabir's mom suddenly started whimpering. She was sobbing when she spoke to Daddy, "Why don't you go and enquire from someone how my son is. My son is just a wall away and I don't even know how he is." He left his seat in an instant. I asked Daddy to sit back. "I will go and enquire." I went to the reception, filled up all the formalities and asked the lady who is to be approached to know about Kabir's health. To which she told me, "Sister D'costa is the head nurse and must be somewhere around the ICU." "Oh, there she is." She said pointing to a nurse who was passing by. She called out to her. The receptionist told her I wanted to know about the accident case who had been admitted the previous night.

"Oh, that boy, he had some injury on the head. Dr Venkatraman has operated on him. He is under observation and there is nothing to worry about. Doctor is operating another patient now. Have you completed the formalities?"

"Yes." I said.

"Okay, then you will be called to the doctor's cabin to speak to him."

"Can we meet him now?"

"No, my dear, not unless the doctor permits."

Sister D'costa was one of those ladies who always spoke to everyone with a lot of compassion. She seemed to empathise with what everyone was going through.

I said "Okay" and left for the cafeteria, which was in the basement. I got two coffees, a packet of cookies and a water bottle. I went to his parents and offered them coffee. They refused in unison.

"Mummy, please. I don't want Kabir to wake up and find any of us in a disturbed state. He is already injured. I don't want anything else to bother him, so please take care of yourself. Have your coffee and cookies too."

Mom said, "If that is the case, then where is your coffee?"

"I'll go and have it. And yes, I met the head nurse, she told me Kabir is fine and has an injury on his head. They have operated on him and as the doctor gets free from an ongoing operation, they will call us to his cabin." I left to have coffee. I rested my head on the chair at the cafeteria and closed my eyes. My body needed some rest. Last night had been horrible and tiring. There was a whirlwind of emotions in my mind. The morning alarm in my phone distracted me. When I saw my cell to turn it off, I saw four missed calls from Daddy. My phone was on silent mode because of which I had missed Daddy's calls. After mom's demise Daddy did not have any specific routine of sleeping and waking up. I guess Daddy was up too early that day and might have called me as he must have realised that I wasn't home. I immediately called him back.

"Nidhi, are you out since night? What have you been up to?"

I told Daddy the whole thing. He said he'll reach hospital asap. Daddy was there in no time.

It was 10:30 am. We were called to the doctor's cabin. There was a team of doctors sitting there. One of them read aloud, 'Kabir Gandhi, is it?'

I said "Yes."

He started, "When he was brought here, he had an injury on the left side of his head and fortunately there were no internal injuries. But even then, since the injury is related to the head, we need to keep him under observation."

"Anything to worry about?" I asked.

"Nothing so far."

Doctors always give such diplomatic answers just to be on the safer side.

"When can we see him?"

"As soon as he regains consciousness, we'll check him once and allow you to see him."

It had been really long since we had been waiting. Daddy requested Kabir's parents to come with him for lunch. They resisted initially but Daddy convinced them somehow. I told them I would have something at the cafeteria and be there in the hospital itself. And I decided to quickly grab a bite from the cafeteria. Kabir never liked when I skipped meals and ignored my health. I rushed, had a burger and came back. I wanted someone to be present when he gained consciousness.

The doctor followed by his team of assistants had come for a round. After a few minutes when they came out, they told me, "you can meet him." My heart was pounding really fast. It was really hard for me to see him in this state. I wanted to hug him so badly. I entered the ICU. His eyes were wide open. He didn't even blink them once in a minute. I went closer, "Baby how are you feeling now?" He did not answer me, nor was he happy when he saw me. It was a bit weird. He started recalling all that had happened the previous night.

He asked me in an aggressive voice, "Where is Rihanna?" His eyes were already red. He scared me with his behaviour.

"Tell me Nidhi where is she? Why aren't you replying?"

Suddenly he started moving violently. Those rapid jerking movements in his body were horrifying. I didn't know if he was facing lots of pain in his body or something else was bothering him. When the sister noticed him, she immediately called the doctor. I was asked to leave the room. Three of them had returned by then. When mom asked me how he was, I was reduced to tears.

I was sniffing when I spoke, "Mom he seemed fine for a while but I don't know what happened to him all of a sudden, there were jerking movements in his body, he was not responding to me, he kept on asking about Rihanna. Daddy please do something; I can't see him like this." Daddy hugged me to console me, "Don't worry *Gudda* I am here, he'll be fine. It is very obvious for him to behave like this, he has been through such a tragic accident. How can he forget everything overnight? Give him some time at least. Stop crying now."

The doctors came out of the room.

I asked them what was happening to Kabir.

"It's very hard for us to come to a conclusion immediately. We need to observe him for the next 48 hours, only then we can speak about it. Till then please bear with us."

Saturday, December 23, 1:00 p.m

"Kabir is experiencing seizures, seizure is a sudden attack of illness, a stroke. There are very wild movements in his body when he becomes violent. But these seizures have nothing to do with his head injury. His wound on the contrary is healing. These seizures are due to the trauma and shock of the girl's death probably. Was she very close to him?"

"Yes." I said

"In medical terms Kabir is suffering from "Non Epileptic Attack Disorder (NEAD)." We are shifting him to a private ward today. And we hope after a few days, the impact of the incident will faint and he'll be fine. You people just make sure that whenever you talk to him, don't remind him of that accident."

Next day I got a huge bunch of flowers, his favourite grilled sandwich, a big smile on my face, wore his favourite coloured dress and hopes in my mind, *Here I come Kabir.*

He was lying on the bed in his ward, his body still, staring at the ceiling.

He noticed me, but didn't greet me.

"Hey Kabir," I said.

No reply.

"See what I've got for you, your favourite grilled sandwich. Come let's eat it."

"Favourite?" he said, still staring at the ceiling, "Rihanna was my favourite...and I have lost her. She could have been saved. She could have lived a beautiful life. If those bastards were human, they should have stopped there. If they wouldn't have rushed to escape, today Rihanna would have been alive."

I went forward to hug him, to console him. He pushed me back vigorously, "I don't need your hug. If you can do anything for me, bring Rihanna back. She was my responsibility when she was with me. I couldn't save her. And I survived. I have no right to live either." He abruptly pulled out the saline pipe from his vein and got down from the bed. He started looking here and there for a solid object to hurt himself. I was petrified.

"Kabir please stop. Please Kabir." I started crying. His actions shook me. I couldn't do anything to help him out. He was throwing things kept in the room out of wrath. Because of the noise, a sister rushed into the room to check what the matter was. When she saw Kabir behaving this way, she immediately called out for her fellow workers. They dragged him to the bed and one of the sisters injected Kabir. As soon as he was injected, he calmed down, and within seconds, fell asleep.

I was trying to avoid any confrontation with daddy. Although I had covered my neck with a scarf even then I didn't want to face daddy. My state of mind was apparent. Anyone could easily figure out that something was wrong with me. The moment I entered home, I saw daddy in the living room. I didn't even greet him and went straight to my room. Instead of resolving it, I added to my problem. I was such a big moron. Daddy wouldn't have enquired otherwise but since I left without having a word with him, he became curious to know what was wrong. When he came in, I had removed my scarf to see the severity of the wound into the mirror. It was not that deep but the bleeding had not stopped. Daddy understood that I was afraid of being questioned, that's why he didn't ask anything.

"Kamla, get the first aid box quickly," he said.

I stood still. Daddy asked me to sit and asked *Kaaki* to clean the wound and apply band aid on it. Daddy's reaction was not even close to what I had anticipated. Instead of hammering me with a number of questions, Daddy behaved calmly.

"I'll send you a glass of warm milk with turmeric, have it. It will help you recover quickly. And take some rest."

"Daddy I am sorry. Please sit Daddy. Actually, I thought of telling you immediately. But then I was scared thinking you may judge Kabir, that's why I decided not to tell you about this. Kabir is not at all in his senses and it was my mistake. He was already disturbed and I was bothering him by constantly asking him what was wrong. He was already going through pain and had just relaxed after a seizure. The room was a complete mess, he had thrown things here and there out of agony. Instead of understanding his plight, I kept on asking him what's wrong as if I didn't know. He lost his temper and threw the fork kept beside him, which accidentally hurt me. It was not at all intentional. I can't see him like this Daddy. I feel helpless. Those bastards…they must be having fun somewhere leaving us in such a mess. How I wish I could have killed them. Sister D'costa told me Kabir behaves this way all the time. They treat him like an animal at times, they tie him up to bring him under control. Those dogs are wandering freely and my innocent Kabir is trapped in this mess."

"Calm down *Gudda*, just calm down. I know Kabir is going through a tough time. I know I can't do much right now, but I will make sure that the culprits are punished and Rihu gets justice Commissioner Sinha has given me his word that I will see them behind bars in a couple of days."

I was astonished knowing that Daddy had already taken steps to find those bastards.

"Daddy you've already spoken to the police?"

"You think I am going to let those bastards live freely? Especially after seeing how their carelessness has affected so many lives?"

"I love you Daddy! Love you a lot."

"I love you too *Gudda*, now cheer up. Everything will be fine. I am always there for you."

Our conversation ended with an affectionate hug.

Time was flying Every day were almost the same. Neither was Kabir's condition improving nor our pain getting any better. Our meetings which otherwise used to be filled with love and passion were now filled with fear and despondency.

January 13, 2018

After coming out of Kabir's ward, I went to see the doctor.

"Nidhi, it's been three weeks since we are trying and expecting progress in Kabir's case. But unfortunately, the medication and efforts are not working towards his progress. He is not able to forget that little girl ummm...what's her name...? Yes, Rihanna. He is not able to forget her, we are giving him medication to prevent the seizures, but the problem is whenever he sees a vehicle, he loses control and we can't keep him unconscious all the time. And we can't imprison him between these four walls forever. If he watches a vehicle on T.V or the mobile phone, he loses control, and sometimes he becomes very violent. He has a constant fear of accidents. Physically he is fine but mentally he is still disturbed. I would suggest you take him to a psychiatrist, a mental health professional. Maybe psychotherapy will work better in this case. Our main concern is, he skips meals and is under constant distress. And on top of this, these seizures. You can even try taking him to a remote village, where he won't come across any vehicle, any discomfort, nor will he remember any gloomy incident. You can help him come out of this and bring him back to normal. I am afraid if this continues, it can lead to a heart attack or maybe he can harm himself which can become fatal. He has tried the latter a couple of times before."

I had to decide what was to be done. Kabir's condition was getting weaker day by day. I was feeling helpless. He had always been my saviour. And now when it was my turn, why was I losing hope? He made impossible things possible for me. He showed me the most beautiful part of life. All the luxuries, money and beauty never made me feel special, it was his love which did that. He filled my shallow life with love and compassion. How could I let him go?

I called Aditi.

"Hey Aditi..."

"Hey Nidhi, how are you and how's Kabir?"

"Aditi, listen to me. I am moving to Chandigarh today; I can't explain why. But in my absence, I want you to update me about Kabir's health."

"But Nidhi, how can you leave him behind in such a condition? You know he won't survive. Is going to Chandigarh more important than Kabir's life? Answer me."

I had no answer.

"Nidhi, are you running away from the situation?" she said with sheer aggression, "Exactly...when he loved you, he was fine, you loved him back. But now that he is not well and dynamic like before, you are kicking him off your life. I must say he loved the wrong girl. He needs you the most now, he is already not able to bear the pain of Rihanna's death, you want to add to his pain by leaving him! Great.

I just can't let you go

Do one thing, why don't you kill him and then go. Anyway, he won't survive for long after you go. What's the point in slowly poisoning him? Kill him at once. And then find someone in Chandigarh!"

"Aditi please! I am doing this for him. Please understand me, I am already exhausted."

Aditi calmed down, somewhere in the corner of her heart she knew abusing me was baseless but she still continued. She did that because she found herself helpless in Kabir's case. She was worried about Kabir and was concerned for him.

"I hope you understand why I've been pressing you to stay back. And I hope what you've thought works well. I will do my bit to help you both. Take care. Bye."

"Bye."

Bhai didn't expect Daddy and me to visit him. He knew the kind of situation that Kabir was in. He knew we could not leave him alone. Our arrival was a big surprise to him. He was astonished when he saw us in the living room. "Nidhi, Daddy I don't believe you are here!" he said in sheer excitement, "I don't believe you made it to join me on my special day."

Daddy and I were confused. *Bhai* probably misunderstood the reason for our visit. But he was not at all at fault. From his point of view, it was an obvious guess that we were there for him, what else could be the reason. *Bhai's* reaction aggravated my problem. I was already apprehensive about how to ask him what I wanted. I couldn't kill his happiness by telling him we were here for some other purpose and not for him. We were here for Kabir. And I couldn't guess Daddy's intent, but I didn't even remember it was his big day tomorrow.

Bhai was having a gala time. He was not even able to hold his excitement till we freshened up and had our breakfast. He wanted to show us the town at the earliest. We joined him for an excursion to the town after we finished eating.

We went in *bhai's* Porsche. Daddy and *bhai* were seated at the front and I was sitting behind. I was only physically present there, I had left my heart and mind with Kabir. Oh Kabir...I was already missing him so much...my baby...I could feel my heart pounding. I eventually ended up with a single question, why? But there was nothing which could justify and answer my questions. All the luxuries, all the lovely people around, it came across as meaningless. No matter how much I pretended to be normal and tried to escape my inner turmoil, the memories bothered me and shattered my confidence.

Bhai guided us throughout our drive inside the town.

As we entered the town, there was a rock waterfall with beautiful bushes around it and the name Vindur was carved on the rocks.

"Look at this waterfall Nidhi, it looks even more gorgeous after sunset because it has submersible spotlights, you will see a splash of lighting with running water, and it looks magical."

He continued as we headed inside.

"We have a huge chunk of open space in the town. These manicured lawns with breathtaking fountains and lush green surroundings make this place no less than heaven. And to add more beauty, we have these pleasing cascade falls, creative swimming pools and serene water bodies.

These interesting walkways will surely encourage people to start walking and jogging. It'll instigate fitness and wellbeing goals in people's minds. In such an environment you will wake up to chirping birds and everything else that adds to a quality living."

Bhai stopped detailing after a while. I realised it was because of my lack of interest. I realised I should have been more reciprocative. And *bhai* was expecting some sort of a reaction from me because Daddy was already aware of all this. I tried to show some interest after that. "*Bhai* what about this mall? You are looking after its management?"

"No *Gudda*, it's not possible for me to personally look after everything. I have a tie up with a company which will take care of its operations. I have tied up with the best companies in the city for gym, club house, hobby clubs, activity centres, electricians, plumbers, maintenance and you won't see anything out of place. Everything is thought out."

"And *bhai* what are these empty spaces for?"

"Ohh these...these are free hold plots for those who want to build their home on their own."

"That's great!! You haven't left a single room for criticism."

"Yeah, we even have spaces for commercial purposes like convenience stores, chemists and super markets. We have created enough room for onsite conveniences."

Bhai regained enthusiasm after my involvement.

"You know Nidhi there would hardly be any need to getaway. This place is completely self- sustainable. We have a boat club, amphitheatre, a boutique hotel, banquets and fine dining restaurants, kids play areas, spas, etc. It's going to be a positive and productive life for its residents. Apart from luxuries we have also taken care of safety, security and convenience. We have 24/7 security and power back up, fire station and fuel station."

"*Bhai* why don't we have a look at one of the apartments from inside?"

"Oh, sure why not?" *bhai* said.

"Come inside *Gudda*, come Daddy," *bhai* said as one of the office employees opened a flat for us.

"Have a look, the opulent interiors are designed to arouse your senses." The flat had a rich wooden flooring, a modular kitchen and super luxurious bath fittings.

It was beautiful beyond my expectations "*Bhai*, it's just wow!" I said

"Yes *Gudda*, it's great. I want buyers to fall in love with their home. It's a perfect dream house." Daddy was extremely proud of what his son had created.

Bhai was elated and full of joyous emotions after hearing our comments.

"Why don't we go and have coffee at our favourite place?" *bhai* asked.

"Why not," Daddy said.

I was neutral and just gave an agreeing nod.

We then left for the café. We ordered nachos and cappuccino.

"How's Kabir, Nidhi?" *bhai* asked.

"He has become really weak, still gets seizures." I was down in the dumps all of a sudden as I recalled Kabir's state. I was so far away from him, almost hoping he could be with us.

"Nidhi why don't you bring him here, maybe the change in place will help him. We have a multi- speciality hospital in the town itself. I forgot to tell you that there are three fully functional schools for your future kids, he said in a funny tone."

I laughed. After so long.

Even Daddy was smiling. Finally, it ended well. But now I was really nervous and tried to gather courage to talk to *bhai* for the purpose we were here.

This township project was *bhai's* dream that had become a reality. People always have that one special thing or person whom they live for. That one dream that does not allow you to sleep, that rules your thoughts. For *bhai* it was this township project. He had spent countless nights staying awake and skipped plenty of meals while working for this project. Many times, he ignored health as well and the flow of work continued. *Bhai* always went extra mile for the successful completion of this project. And at this crucial time, I was about to give him the shock of his life. I felt like standing on pins and needles, I didn't know how to bring it up, after all it was a tall ask. But I had to open up, now or later. At the dinner table I took this audacious step to ask bhai...

"*Bhai* I want this township."

Initially bhai was a little surprised, he took a big pause and then said, "Everything we have is all yours *Gudda*."

"You are not getting me bhai. I want to take control of this project and make some changes in it."

"Changes? But in the morning when I showed you the whole town, daddy and you found it perfect. In fact, I remember you saying, 'it was just exceptional and beyond your dreams', then what changed suddenly? But if what you want to say is actually worth changing then I will definitely do it, tell me."

"*Bhai* I want to ban vehicles in the town for the time being," I said in a nervous tone.

Bhai had a bite in his mouth which he immediately swallowed, listening to what I said. He took a napkin to wipe his lips, kept his fork aside and then said, "Ban vehicles? What makes you think of something so impractical? This is absurd. In today's fast life how can someone even think of living without vehicles. And this is not a small society where the exit is just a minute's walk away. This is a big town, spread over 400 acres, a small city in itself. Walking to the exit would be a big task."

"*Bhai* I know, people can use cycles, in fact we will provide them cycles for all the members of family. And it would even prove beneficial for their health."

Bhai was now getting really angry. His tone had turned a bit harsh, "But why, why do we even have to do this? What the hell is the logic behind banning vehicles?"

"For humanism *bhai*, for Kabir."

"Okayyy...the picture is now clear to me. You have gone mad; you have lost your senses now. But do you even realise what you are doing, you are using a sledgehammer to crack a nut. Just to cure your boyfriend I am not putting my dreams and several years of hard-earned money at stake."

"*Bhai* please, just for a few months. As people start realising the benefits, they will avoid vehicles willingly. Trust me."

"Nidhi I've never raised a hand against you but now I seriously feel like it, and before I lose control, stop this nonsense!" he said this in a very aggressive tone. "And daddy why don't you explain to this stupid girl, what she is asking is ridiculous."

Daddy now began to speak. I did not have any clue of what he was going to say. "Sarth first of all calm down. Anger is not at all good for your health. And I go along with Nidhi's thoughts."

"But Daddy!" *bhai* shouted.

"Let me complete, Sarth."

"Sorry." he said with his eyes facing the ground.

"This is what even your mother had always tried to do. Explain to everyone the worth of other people, to bring harmony. She always tried sowing humanism in everyone's mind all her life and even died trying the same."

I was bewildered hearing what daddy said. This was the first time after mom's demise I had heard about the reason for her death. I wanted to know the whole thing. I had given up on this topic long back but now that daddy had turned over a new leaf, I had become curious.

"Daddy please, please tell me the whole thing." I pleaded before daddy, "I really want to know what happened to mom. I promise I will be able to handle it. You know that I've changed, I've learnt to deal with the hardships of life. The experiences in the recent past have made me tougher, like I was never before. Please daddy."

Daddy made up his mind to tell me the whole thing. I thought it was only me who had been kept in the dark, but even *bhai* was not aware of the whole thing. Daddy began, avoiding eye contact with us.

"It was 10 p.m. I was waiting for her to come back so we could eat dinner together. She had gone to Vindur. Whenever we were in Pune, she went to Vindur daily, sometimes just for five minutes, or if she had ample time, she spent the whole day over there. That day she knew I was waiting for her, so I was sure she would be back any moment. I gave her a call, to enquire where she was and also because I was missing her."

She answered, "Hi honey."

"Hi, where have you reached?"

"How did you know I've already left?"

"Ohh come on! You are talking as if we've met yesterday. I've known you for years. I know how particular you are about your commitments; you had promised me we'll have dinner together. So, I knew you must have already left. Haven't you?"

"Yes, I have. I am waiting to reach home and be with my dear husband."

"You always know how to pamper me. What would I do without you?"

"Hey, hey you...stop you bastard," she started shouting vigorously and hung up my call abruptly.

I got very worried and called her back.

"Honey I'll call you in a while, don't worry, everything is okay. Please hang up now."

I had to ask her what exactly made her shout like this. Was she safe? What was wrong. But all I could helplessly say was " Okay, please call me back as soon as possible."

While Meera was talking to me on call, three guys travelling in a land cruiser overtook her car from the wrong side which made her very cautious and alert. She was sensing something wrong could happen, and it actually did. The guys were drunk and out of control which was the reason they overtook Meera's car from the wrong side. There was a slum dwelling on the road side. They were driving the car very rashly because of which the boy lost control and the speeding car smashed the legs of two people who were lying on the pavement. This was outrageous for Meera. Her wrath knew no bounds. Many passing vehicles and people standing around promptly reached out to help the injured. Meera was quite sure that they would receive help and she felt she should instead follow those bastards and teach them a lesson. Even if the injured got treated, some of them would probably not be able to live a normal life again. Already they were deprived of so many basic needs. Physical disability would hamper their living even more. Meera was an exuberant and courageous woman. She did not leave any stone unturned in chasing the boys. The boys were already shattered with what they did and wanted to escape as soon as possible. When they saw Meera's car following them, it was a matter of great twitchiness for them. They started discussing what had to be done next to avoid the situation from getting worse for them. Meanwhile Meera overtook the car and stationed her car parallel to their car, preventing their car from moving forward. They stopped their car abruptly. For once they thought of leaving the car and breaking out but got a little calm when they saw just one lady coming out of the car. Just one lady chasing them was a blessing in disguise for the guys. They instantly dropped the idea of running. Meera was bold enough and started heading fearlessly towards the boys. As soon as she reached the car, she opened the door of the driver's seat and gave the boy a smack on his cheeks. She pulled the boy out holding him by his collar with one hand and by his arm with the other hand. She slapped him again furiously. She started speaking vigorously and while she was speaking the boy's collar was still in her hand.

"What the hell did you guys just do? You crushed so many people under your car and instead of stopping there and helping them out, you just left as if nothing happened. I am not going to spare you guys. You will pay for this. I'll make sure you guys are punished severely so that you repent for your mistake!" She said in great anger.

A boy from inside the car said, "Hey Atul, this bitch is barking a lot. Let's take her into the car and we'll teach her a lesson." Meera had not expected this to happen at all, her eyes widened with fear. The other two guys came out of the car, one of them closed her mouth with his hand to constrain her from shouting. Both of them together pushed her into the car. The boy who was driving took his seat. As Meera had blocked their way by parking her car in front of theirs, he took a quick u-turn and left. The guys started assaulting Meera.. She kept on shouting for help, the car was too fast for anyone to hear to Meera's cries. She pleaded before them to leave her. But they were drunk and continued touching her in a lecherous manner. Meera was 48 years of age but she looked much younger;. she had maintained her figure very well. But these guys being drunk and Meera being aggressive with them was the reason this happened. She had hurt their fake ego. Meera made every effort to save herself but she failed. She made a final effort and succeeded in opening the door. She first pushed one of the boy's out of the car and then she jumped out. The boy was hit real bad when he was thrown from the car. But what happened to Meera was the most unfortunate part. As she jumped out of the car, she was smashed by a truck. I did not receive your mom's body; I received her body in parts."

There was complete silence and then all three of us burst into tears.

"Sarth, your mother will be very happy if we succeed in this plan. Allow Nidhi, please."

Daddy folded his hands before *bhai*, "Please."

Bhai was left with no option but to agree. If the secret of mom's death would have been told to me earlier, I would surely have been shattered, but now it gave me strength, it gave me a purpose.

A grand party was organised the next day for the successful completion of the township project. All the VIPs of the city were invited. A short promotional video was to be played detailing the town. Many flats were already booked and the rest were expected to be booked after this party. But now that *bhai* knew I was going to make this announcement, he had completely lost hopes for the rest of the flats being booked. On the contrary, he was worried about the previous bookings too. He felt nobody would want a home with such rules around. Bhai was sure that now he would have to face a lot of allegations. He was trying to prepare himself for that. The time had come. *Bhai* was looking very nervous. He had not even thought in his wildest dreams, that his special day would turn out the way it had. I had no words to console him. The night before the party I had been working on a small video presentation. Through the video, people would know the reason behind the announcement of banning vehicles in town. I was supposed to play it after *bhai's* official video of the township project. Bhai's video manifested all the details of this beautiful piece of land. The room was filled with applause after the video ended and then another video started, the one which I had worked on.

In the video; a small kid is seen running on the street and his grandpa behind him with a stick in his hand to support him. Then the image changes, a man is reading a newspaper sitting on his rocking chair on the balcony. The headlines read, 'Chandigarh: Pedestrian killed after being hit by a jeep in Kurali. Victim was a 22 year old boy who was the only son to his parents, and was the only earning source of the family.'

Another one said: 'Chandigarh, car crashes on the divider on Amritsar-Jalandhar highway. 3 dead, 1 injured.'

A series of headlines were presented.

'Maharashtra: 3 college girl students riding two-wheelers killed in mishap.'

'Tamil Nadu: Six killed as a car rams into an auto rickshaw.'

'Mumbai: 4 injured after Jaguar rams into 10 vehicles, locals caught hold of the driver.'

The image changed, a lady was watching a video which she received on a whatsapp group. The video showed a cctv footage of an accident where a lady was killed who had delivered a baby six months ago.

"These tragic news pieces show us the bitter reality and compel us to think where the world is going wrong. Whenever our loved one is out of home, we pray for them to return home safely. I want to remove that fear from your mind. I want to assure you all that if a twenty-one-year old son's daddy is sitting at home, there are many other daddies who will take care of him when he is out. Banning vehicles is not the only measure to be taken. It's also going to ignite humanism and concern amongst all of us. A son won't worry about his old father when he is out for a walk. There are many sons around who will look after him. A small kid can play freely without the fear of accidents or being kidnapped. Everyone will live for each other. When you don't have a medium to travel far and wide for entertainment, you'll certainly look for it around you. And why do you actually need to travel long distances? This town is sufficient with all the luxuries, necessities, entertainment and each and every amenity needed to live a happy life. We just want to make it safe, we want to make it a home. A big family."

The presentation came to an end.

I was behind the mic, "I, Nidhi Dhillon, announce that there won't be any vehicles allowed in the town except cycles and a few indoor solar cars for those who are unable to ride cycles. These cars are perfect for short distance transportation. The compact shape and lightweight construction of the cars make them the safest to travel on streets. Each and every family member of Vindur will be gifted a cycle. You won't find a need to go out of the town, nevertheless there are exit points at every short distance, from where you can drive your vehicles out. There will be a red light on every balcony. If someone lights up the LED, that will indicate that they need help. An old couple who is living alone, left by their kids won't have to worry anymore. They have a big family, Vindur. Treat everybody the way you wish for others to treat you."

I took a big pause, there was complete silence.

"That's all, thank you."

One of the guests started the applause followed by a big round of applause.

Those shining eyes and smiles told me that the idea was accepted and loved.

'Something to happen which never happened before.'

'Dhillon's Vindur aspiring city emerging with safe homes and safer environment.'

'Vindur expected to invite bids'

'Looking for a dream home, Vindur is the place for you'

'Vindur is something, society has been looking forward to since forever'

These were the headlines of the next day.

The following week *bhai* was supposed to give possessions. He had received innumerable calls, mails and messages asking when he would begin the bidding. Bhai felt overwhelmed. I was really happy for him. Bhai already ordered the cycles and solar cars and asked them to be delivered at the earliest. He personally monitored the fixing of LEDs. Unlike me, *bhai* was been busy all day long. I was just sitting idle and missing Kabir. I had so many reasons to be happy, but I felt miserable from within. It was because my Kabir was far away from me. He felt like blood in my veins. I always wanted him with me. I called Aditi to ask about him. She said Kabir was really curious, he desperately wanted to know where I was. Kabir was really worried about me, he was just hoping and praying that I was fine and was not in any trouble. His love and concern for me, diverted his mind from Rihanna to me. Aditi gave a single answer to all his questions, 'I don't know.'

After that party *bhai*, Daddy and I directly met at the dinner table. Three of us exchanged smiles.

"Nidhi my joy knows no bounds, the flats are being booked at fast speed that too at a price higher than expected. When are you going to bring Kabir over here?" *bhai* asked.

"*Bhai* let people start residing, only then."

"It will take a week or two, will he be fine by then?"

"I really hope so."

"I would suggest you move to the penthouse."

"But *bhai* you had exclusively designed that for yourself, how can I stay there?"

"Oh, come on Gudda! Does it make a difference? I'll be equally happy if you both live there. And anyways I wouldn't have moved in right away. I had just kept it ready for the sake of it. It's a beautiful house. You start shifting your stuff from today itself. And yes, I think you shouldn't shift Kabir's stuff from Pune. Better buy all new things for him."

It was a little awkward to talk about me and Kabir sharing the house before marriage, especially in front of daddy. Marriage was anyways a formality. I was already Kabir's and he was mine. Even then the situation was a little tricky. But I felt relaxed when daddy said, "yes *Gudda*, Sarth is right you go shopping for Kabir and make sure you buy each and every thing which he may need. Sarth why don't you go help her out."

"Daddy I am very busy," *bhai* said.

I quickly said, "It's okay daddy I'll go on my own and anyways it's not going to get completed in a day or two. It will take a few days, better I'll start tomorrow and take bhai along as and when he is free."

Daddy just gave a nod.

"Bhai tomorrow morning I want to see the penthouse first, so that if I need anything for the house, I will shop for that too ."

"Sure, morning we'll leave together. I'll show you the penthouse and leave for the office after that."

I just kept changing sides that night, I was very restless. Many times I thought of messaging Kabir or at least calling him. But then I thought if this curiosity is helping him to recover, I'll have to bear this brunt of separation. I then promised to myself that I won't call or message him unless and until I bring him here. I knew it was not going to be easy at all. But I had to do this. I kept on scrolling his pictures on my cell phone, then started reading our old conversations. Soon I was lost in his memories. His hugs, his kisses, his endearments, the way he used to call me ' oh madam', and how he was my biggest weakness. I was missing his long breaths around my neck. His memories brought tears into my eyes. I was helplessly in love with him.

I was really happy shopping for him. I was enjoying doing it. Decorating our home, buying stuff for him. Our room was full of our pictures to remind him of all the beautiful moments we spent together. I wanted him to see them and feel only love when he came there. I wanted to pamper him, wanted to make him feel like the most special person on this planet. My baby...I wanted to kiss him all over. Could not wait to get him here. Everything was almost settled. The penthouse was ready. People had inhabited some of the flats. It was time to bring him here. I was so excited for that day. I was planning to bring him here with whole hearted enthusiasm. Before I could go there to get him, there was an emergency. The enthusiasm was killed and replaced with fears. Fear of losing him. I received a call from Aditi. She was whimpering. Her cries sank my heart. With a palpitating heart I asked her, "Aditi what's wrong? Is it about Kabir? Tell me for heaven sake."

"Yes Nidhi...Rah...Kabir..." she was stammering, gasping for breath as she spoke.

"Nidhi that bitch Mahira had come to the hospital to see him. Kabir had a beautiful smile on his face. He was holding your picture in his arms. He was hugging it with all his love. Out of envy, she said, 'Kabir I am really sorry for all that has happened. Your condition, and that poor girl's death. I feel really sad for you. But you know what when you are into wrong hands, wrong things happen to you. It's all because of your relationship with Nidhi. For her, for her love you always went out of the way. And love which was not even real. If she really loved you she wouldn't have fled away. I know she hasn't even called you once after escaping, how will she? She has no answers to your questions due to which she is hiding.'"

"Where were you Aditi when she was talking all this rubbish to him?"

"She deliberately sent me to the parking lot, saying that she has probably left the car's window open and that she has a diamond bracelet in the car dashboard. I was unaware of her intentions so I readily agreed. When I was back, I saw the room full of broken glass pieces and blood. The nurse told me that he had hit his wrist and elbow. He has got stitches on his hand. He had come out of Rihanna's pain with great difficulty. Mahira refreshed those memories. And because of all this he got a panic attack. It had been a week since he was free from these attacks. He is injured and disturbed. What do I do Nidhi? Please come back."

"Listen Aditi, get the discharge papers ready, ask the doctors for all the dos and don'ts very carefully. I will come and take him with me."

"But Nidhi, it's gonna be a long journey, do you think it will be safe for him.'

"I'll take him in my Daddy's chopper, don't worry about that. You just speak to the doctors about preventive measures and safety instructions and don't leave him alone even for a single second till I come. I will call his mom and speak to her about this."

Convincing his mom was not a big task.

And Daddy not only agreed to bring him in his chopper, he came along with me. Doctors suggested taking him in an unconscious state to avoid any disturbance to his mind. No one was sure of his reaction of travelling to a new city. So, it was better to keep him unconscious while travelling. We safely reached our house. Daddy was tired of the journey and he tried his best to provide us our own space. He immediately left after leaving Kabir in his room. Daddy asked kabir's nurse to stay in a floor below our penthouse, to be easily available in case of emergency.

It was a treat to my eyes watching him in sound sleep. I sat down on the bed and I was staring at him. It was such a relief, he was finally with me. I could not stop myself from hugging him. I went straight into his blanket and hugged him very tight. I took his hands and rolled them around my waist, soon he tightened the grip. He was out of his sleep. I was expecting a lot of questions from him. But I was wrong. How could I forget that we both were in the same boat. If I was going crazy missing him over here, even he had been longing for me. If I was burning in pain, he was burning too and in fact with much deeper pain. At least I was aware of his situation, he was completely unaware of what was going on with me. I realised how badly he wanted this warmth. We silently enjoyed each other's warmth. He held back the questions but could not hold back the tears.

"Where have you been, baby? Where were you all this while?"

I sucked his tears from his cheeks, I started kissing him all over his face.

I did not bother to answer him, I just wanted to feel him. We had never been wild in bed, our intimacy had always been full of compassion and calm. That day he kissed me wildly for the first time. He was nibbling my lips. His loud heaves had set my heart on fire. His hand was on my waist, pulling me closer towards him.

"I love you Kabir...love you a lot baby...I can't tell you how badly I have missed you...I was craving so desperately for your touch, your warmth...baby you mean the world to me. I can't even imagine my life without you. In Fact, I can't even imagine a day without you anymore. Now that you are with me, I won't ever let you go, just be mine for today, tomorrow and forever."

He kissed me again, kept kissing me. That day we made love thrice in four hours.

"Get up Kabir, you need to eat something now. You have to take your medicines then."

"Medicines!" He said in a very low voice.

"Ya baby. You have to."

"Jaan, nothing will get better with these medicines. You know what I am going through."

"Of course, I know and who else can know it better than me? Trust me with my love and a few medicines you will be my old Kabir again."

"Don't love me so much Nidhi. I can't give you anything. I can never be your old Kabir again. How can you love a person and think of living with him, for whom even going to the washroom by himself was a task a few days ago?"

I just went closer to him and kept my hand on his lips to stop him from saying anything else.

"No more bad memories Kabir. Come let's watch a movie."

I was trying to divert his mind, that's why I thought of watching a movie.

We were watching a romantic movie and ended up making love. The urge of being together was so strong that we were actually together, was still unbelievable for both of us.

Kabir's condition had started improving. He had even started regaining weight, which he had lost in the past few weeks. We had spent a whole week at home. He was afraid of even going out to the balcony. Although Rihanna's face was not flashing in front of his eyes as much as it used to before. Even then he did not have the courage to move out. Our routine was sex-sleep-wake up-sex-eat-watch movies-eat-sleep-cuddle and so on. Nothing else except this. The movies I chose for him to watch used to be either romantic or inspiring. I wanted to ensure that no scene in the movie aggravated his pain. One day we were watching a movie in our room. He was lying on my lap and I was moving my hand in his hair.

"You need a haircut baby, and shave too."

"I am not going out anywhere jaan."

"Okay then I'll give you a shave and a haircut."

"What?"

"Ya, so what?"

"You don't know how to do it."

"I know I can't do it professionally but I know the basics at least and anyway if I spoil your hair, you are not going out so no big deal. No one is going to point it out."

"Are you serious Nidhi?"

"I am, baby, now get up let's get started."

I asked one of our employees to get all the material needed.

The material required for a haircut and shave was with us in no time.

As I opened the stuff, there were band aids in it too.

I didn't ask him why he had got band aids.

Kabir burst out laughing while I was still puzzled.

"What Kabir? Tell me or else I am going to kill you."

"Jaan he must have anticipated in advance that you will hurt my cheeks with a razor. And what else can we expect from a noob."

The whole room was filled with laughter. I just wanted to see him happy like that for days to come. I loved watching him laugh.

"C'mon Kabir you think I can hurt you with this," I said in a kiddish tone.

"No baby I don't doubt. I am sure you will."

I gave him a tough naughty look, "In any case, I am doing it. Come to the balcony."

"Balcony, why balcony. Why not here?"

He was resisting, he wanted to avoid the scene of the hustle bustle on the road. But I wanted him to see that these streets are not the same, this world is not the same. I would have explained to him about all that but I wanted him to see it on his own. I invited him saying that there is not enough light in the room and I may seriously hurt him. But he agreed only when I said he had to come out for my sake.

When I was shaving out his beard he said, "Jaana you know what? They give a shower also after shaving in good saloons."

I knew he was teasing me, I thought of joining him.

"So?"

"So even you should."

"So, you want me to give you a shower?"

"Of course!"

I went closer to his ears and mumbled, "You will have to pay for it, baby."

He pulled me from my waist and made me sit on his lap and said, "I am ready."

"Okay then."

"What okay then? Tell me what you want for it."

"I'll ask for it but not now, later. Only if you are satisfied with my salon services sir."

He smiled.

When we were done with his shaving, we went for a shower. He kept gazing at me for long...

"Stop it Kabir don't look at me like this."

"What?' He said teasing me, then where should I look?"

"Look somewhere else. Do all that you want but don't look at me, I am feeling shy baby."

"How can I love you without looking at you?"

"I don't know," I buried my head in his shoulder.

He then lifted me in his arms and took me to the bathtub.

I just can't let you go

I was lost in his arms, "I love you Kabir."

"Love you much more Nidhi."

I was really hungry after bathing.

"Kabir I am starving to death."

"Come I'll feed you with my hands today."

"I want to have Chinese baby."

"But the cook has already left, hasn't she?"

"Yes, she prepared lunch and left."

"Now what? I don't know how to prepare it, else I would have surely done it for you."

"Don't bother. We'll go out and have it."

He hesitated.

"You had promised to pay me back baby. Now be a gentleman and stand true to your promise, get up and get ready."

"Nidhi how can you forget the way I behaved with you in the hospital that too not once, so many times. Now everything is going well, please don't let the animal in me come out."

"Baby how many days will you cage yourself inside these four walls? One day we have to move on. And we are doing it today. Now come on get ready quickly I am starving."

His eyes were filled with tears. He brought me closer to hug me.

"I am sorry honey, for the way I had behaved, the stress I have given you. But you did not give up on me, I am so blessed to have fallen in love with someone like you."

Manah

"Who told you I did that for you, you don't know how selfish I am, I didn't do it for you. I did it all for myself because I wanted you with me, to love me, to pamper me, to bear with my tantrums."

"I promise to pamper you all my life, to take in your tantrums, to love you with all my heart."

Even I had tears in my eyes, tears of joy!

He wiped them off instantly, "I will never let a tear roll down your eyes as long as I am alive."

I hugged him tight.

"Now get up. Let's go and eat."

"Okay let's go."

We reached the ground floor via lift, as the door opened, I was the first to move out of it. Kabir was behind me, he held my hand to refrain me from going ahead.

"Are you sure Nidhi?"

I pulled him out of the lift.

"Yes, I am baby. Now come."

Kabir was bewildered, the empty parking lot left him confused. He didn't ask me, he silently followed me, "Here this is my bike." I said, pointing towards my bicycle.

"Kabir you ride, I want to sit here in the front, will you take me for a classic long drive?"

Kabir smirked. We were missing the day of the cycle rally. "It was a beautiful memory Kabir, wasn't it?" I said.

"Yes baby. It certainly was."

We started our ride on the bicycle and headed towards a Chinese restaurant in the township itself. All the way Kabir

I just can't let you go

kept noticing the streets filled with cycles and not even a single vehicle. He was confused as to what was happening. When we reached the restaurant, it was almost full but the parking lot didn't have a single vehicle.

"Nidhi, will you please tell me what's happening?"

"Let's go in, order something, and then talk."

He just nodded in acceptance.

We went in, quickly placed the order and we began talking. "Jaana I am sure you are responsible for all the strange things I see around. Aren't you?"

I was confused. I didn't know how he would react. I didn't want to take a chance. I kept quiet.

He repeatedly kept asking me.

I had to tell him before he lost his temper.

His hands were on the table. I took his hand, held his hand in mine and started rubbing it with the other to soothe him. I kissed his hand.

"Kabir we are not in Pune. We are in Chandigarh. This is the township my brother built. And ..." I took a pause.

"And?"

"And I have banned vehicles in this township."

His eyes widened with astonishment.

"What? Banned vehicles! I am sure it isn't that easy. I mean why did you do this...how did you do this?"

He became loud, "Do you even realise what you have done? Just for my sake you have taken such a big step. What if this decision fails? I won't be able to see anyone accusing you."

His voice suddenly lowered, "Why did you do this? You should have left me to my fate."

"Baby if I asked you the same. If I asked you to let me go, to leave me to my fate when I was in the darkest phase of my life, would you?"

"Never."

"Then how can you expect me to do that? And banning vehicles is not only for your good. It's eventually good for every resident here. We are creating a safe environment to live in, that's it. Don't worry, you and I together will turn out the odds into even, cheers!"

"Hope so."

"And now if my highness permits me, can I eat?"

"Oh, I am so sorry honey I didn't realise the food had already arrived."

He fed me the first bite.

After we finished having our food, we were ambling through the town hand in hand. That day fortunately the climate was also magical. The sky had turned orange. The tender cool breeze touching us felt like a different world. It was no less than a fairy tale. The place was already a piece of beauty, the climate added to it. As the daylight was subsiding, the weather was getting colder. I was holding his hands in mine. I wanted to stop time. I would have no regrets in life even if the journey of my life ended there in his arms. Kabir was overwhelmed with what I did for him. He was falling short of words to express it.

"Nidhi you look so beautiful in this twilight, you are no less than a princess. You are my queen."

"Who would have been incomplete without her king," I said kissing his forehead.

Having a look around the town Kabir said, "Nidhi your brother's work is truly commendable. He has created wonders."

I responded with the broadest smile possible.

He pointed towards a balcony, "Oh what's that? The red LED lightning in the balcony looks weird amidst the otherwise beautiful township."

"Oh god, we need to rush, come fast."

'What? But what happened?'

"This light indicates someone needs help inside the house, I said pulling his hand to rush to that particular flat."

The door was closed but the window was fortunately open.

We saw an old man lying on the floor yearning for breath. It was evident that the man was suffering from some illness and was in a very bad condition at that moment. Soon many others too gathered at the door. I asked the man inside, "Uncle please tell me the code of your door lock so that we can break in."

Gasping for breath he said, '5652.'

We opened the door in an instant and went in to help him.

Kabir lifted uncle to the sofa with the help of two other boys who had also come for rescue seeing the red LED light. One of the boys behind said, 'I'll call for the ambulance immediately.'

"No...no beta", uncle said, in a slow-paced voice. He was a rugged old man. "Don't call for the ambulance just get me my inhaler. It must be somewhere in the kitchen." I rushed in the kitchen to get it and fortunately found it in an instant. Soon after using his inhaler, uncle was feeling much better and was in a position to talk and explain what exactly happened to him.

"Thank you so much, all of you for being here to help me out. I stay alone in this flat. Was cooking and suddenly felt suffocated due to the steam in the kitchen. That's why I came into the living room." He took a sigh of relief, "Today's incident reminded me of my olden days where everyone was just a shout away from you. Our homes used to be so small and close that we never felt alone. I remember once when one of our aunts in the neighbourhood was bitten by a venomous snake. She immediately started screaming for help. At that time she was alone at home. I was very young then. We didn't own any vehicles. During those days., vehicles were a luxury. Now-a-days it has become a necessity or precisely speaking a basic necessity. Taking her to the hospital on a bicycle wouldn't have saved her life. My mom was smart enough to cut that particular part with a blade where the snake had bit. She sterilised the blade first to avoid any infection. She then cut it deep to allow the blood to flow out which was contaminated with the snake's poison. We took her to a doctor. She survived just because my mom was there to help her at the spur of the moment. Today I feel the same. I really feel like blessing that girl with all the happiness possible who created this environment here. Today it was me but tomorrow it can be you, your loved ones. Each and every blob you take will someday contribute to the biggest good of the world and will be useful to everyone. And each blob you contribute will come to you in quintals. Instead of sowing luxuries and money, which reap you insecurities and tensions, sow compassion and humanity, which will reap you happiness. At the end of the day, at the end of life, what matters won't be your luxuries and the number of cars you own, it would be how happy you and your loved ones are, don't wait for some angel to come and be your saviour, be one instead. And it's not only about accidents and vehicles. It's about humanism. Till the time these accidents were mistakes, they were acceptable, but today more accidents are a consequence of deliberate irresponsibility and overconfidence. They happen because many of us do not consider the person before us as our own."

Everyone was listening to uncle very keenly. His experience helped all to understand the essence of life. We were so lost in his words that no one remembered to turn off the alerting LED because of which a huge number of people had gathered there. All those listening to uncle were touched by his thoughts. Those thoughts then spread from one person to another and gradually to all.

Kabir was overwhelmed with all that had happened. He was now content. Finally, a world was created where everyone was your own. Health was a priority, crime reduced to almost nil. Girls felt safe. The type of world mom and Kabir wanted.

People in the town shared their thoughts, talents and experiences in the amphitheatre. Most of the people in town never felt the need to go out of town. Scenic beauty, entertainment, education everything was readily available. This LED not only helped uncle that day, it helped many more after that. And the effect of that help was such that it lasted for long in everyone's mind. Vehicles which used to be a basic necessity, were now out of the list of even luxuries. It's not that people in town never used their vehicles but inadvertent use of vehicles had reduced.

One night, I was lying in Kabir's arms, with a sense of relief and comfort, he abruptly woke up.

"Baby what happened, was it a nightmare."

I was really scared if he had had a bad dream. Although he seemed fine the last few days, I was still afraid.

He then said, "That night when I wanted to meet you, when I met with the accident…"

"Baby please don't think of it, it's gone, please."

He said, "Come out with me."

"Where? What happened? Please tell me Kabir."

He took me down, it was midnight.

The streets were empty, although the town was completely safe and secure, I was afraid. Afraid of what Kabir would do next.

He suddenly started doing something on his phone.

I was really confused at what actually was happening.

He then played a song and said, "It was this song that I wanted to dedicate to you that night. Our story would have been incomplete without it."

He turned the blues into blossoms.

I got tears in my eyes, I pushed him a little saying, "You scared me…" and then I hugged him.

We then ambled around listening to the song…

'Here I am this is me
There's nowhere else on earth I'd rather be
Here I am it's just me and you
Tonight, we make our dreams come true

It's a new world it's a new start
It's alive with the beating of young hearts
It's a new day it's a new plan
I've been waiting for you
Here I am
Here I am
Here we are we've just begun
And after all this time our time has come
Ya here we are still going strong
Right here in the place where we belong
It's a new world it's a new start
It's alive with the beating of young hearts
It's a new day it's a new plan
I've been waiting for you
Here I am
Yeah here I am
Here I am, yeah
Yeah here I am
Waiting for you
Here I am this is me
There's nowhere else on earth I'd rather be
Here I am it's just me and you
Tonight, we make our dreams come true
It's a new world it's a new start
It's alive with the beating of young hearts
It's a new day it's a new plan
I've been waiting for you
It's a new world it's a new start

It's alive with the beating of young hearts
It's a new day it's a new plan
I've been waiting for you
Here I am
here I am
(Oh, here I am) right next to you
(Oh, here I am) and suddenly the world is all brand new
Here I am
(Oh, oh, oh)
Here I am
I'm gonna stay
There's nothing standing in our way
Oh, here I am
(Here I am)
Here I am
This is me…'

www.ingramcontent.com/pod-product-compliance
Ingram Content Group UK Ltd.
Pitfield, Milton Keynes, MK11 3LW, UK
UKHW042001230426